The Doppelganger

Trilogy (The Unofficial Minecraft Adventure Short Stories)

Mark Mulle

PUBLISHED BY:

Mark Mulle

Copyright © 2014

Disclaimer
This is a work of fiction. Names, characters, businesses, places, events and incidents are either the products of the author's imagination or used in fictitious manny. Any resemblance to actual persons, living or dead, or actual events is purely coincidental.

Author's Note: These short stories are for your reading pleasure. The characters in this "Minecraft Adventure Series" such as Steve, Endermen or Herobrine...etc are based on the Minecraft Game coming from Minecraft ®/TM & © 2009-2013 Mojang / Notch

Table of Contents

Book One - Steve's Chance

Chapter One

He had made it out on his own at last. Realizing this made him smile and jump for joy and almost made him wonder if it was a dream, but it wasn't. When he stared at the house he had built, it was all too real. It wasn't the fanciest house, and Steve didn't consider himself an architect by any means. The chimney looked a little misaligned, the windows a bit low, but it was livable, which was what Steve honestly cared about at the moment. He was away from his hometown and ready to start anew, a boy slowly becoming a man.

Steve had always wanted to move out of his one-horse town, but he also wanted to have a home in the country. So he built his house right outside the expansive town of Chance, where opportunity was said to thrive. He'd have plenty of room to build a farm and make a garden, all while actually having something to do and job offers unlike his hometown of Daint.

Steve walked inside his house. He still needed to buy or make some furniture. He had brought his bed from his home, but the bed was worn out. Just like he needed a fresh start, he desired a fresh bed as well.

Steve looked around in his room, noticing the single picture that was hanging on the wall. Despite the fact that he left his family and wanted to go his own way, he wanted a reminder of who had raised him. In the picture was Steve, his parents holding his hands. Steve was just a child then, and he wasn't even looking directly in the frame. Instead he was looking down at a pig that had passed through. This was really the only childhood photo he had on him. According to his parents, they lost most of the photos in an unforeseen accident. They wouldn't elaborate, but Steve never asked. He assumed that his parents were upset over losing his most precious photos.

Steve would return to visit his parents someday, but for now he wanted to make his own life. He looked at his house some more, seeing what it needed. It needed a kitchen, that was for sure, as well as some food. Well, he could probably handle the food part, as the food stands were usually at the entrance of Chance. So Steve got out and started going to Chance. His stomach was growling, and he needed some nourishment. He saw the town in the distance. It had some fairly tall buildings and even a giant structure at the end where the ruler resided. The whole town was enclosed by a wall, so he looked for the gate. Once he saw it, he approached the two guards in front of it.

"Say, you look a bit familiar. Did you come here recently?" one of the guards asked.

Steve shook his head. "No, sir. I've just arrived."

"Well, our eyes must be playing tricks on us then. Carry on." The guards opened the gate, and Steve was left scratching his head. He guessed that there were people who resembled him. He didn't stand out or anything with his short brown hair and plain shirt. He was just an ordinary-looking man and probably would be confused with others in the average people out there. He just shrugged as he went inside.

The town was bustling, and he realized he'd get lost in the crowd. For now, he just went to the sides and went to the various stands. A salesman was pitching about how his apples were the crispest around. Steve bought a few and went to the other sellers. He bought some potatoes, tomatoes, and even bought some seeds so he could grow his own things when the time was right. With everything done, Steve went outside of the town and sat on a nearby hill to have his own picnic. He'd rather prepare his food, but eating it raw was good as well. He grabbed the apple and started munching on it. It was actually very sweet and juicy. Was it the best apple ever? Probably not, but it lived up to his expectations. He also ate a tomato as well.

All this time, he looked at Chance. It would be his new home, and he realized that his future would probably depend on the town as well. He wanted to have a career that wouldn't lead him to a dead end, a career that would help him meet people whom he didn't have to force into his life, who actually had things in common with him. He couldn't wait to see all that it had to offer. Chance would be, well, his chance.

Steve went home and put his stash of food away. There was still a lot to be done at this place, and he quickly got to work. He had brought plenty of materials and was quite experienced in crafting things from them. He managed to create his own stove, cabinet, and even table. He also made a small seat for the living room and managed to get a fire going once he got hungry again. He boiled some potatoes and added a bit of tomato sauce to them. As he sat on his newly crafted table, he started to eat them, savoring the taste. He needed some more food, like some meat, bread, and milk, but for now this would suffice.

Once the sun started to set, he made sure that his house was completely closed off to prevent mobs. As he went to bed, he was glad that he was home, but despite his earlier dismissal, he was wondering who the person who looked like him was. Was there another version of him around? If so, Chance had gotten better than ever. He'd love to go on adventures with his twin and be his best friend. As he went to sleep, he slept with a smile on his face.

Chapter Two

When Steve awoke, he almost wanted to work on his house some more, but he knew that he should go to Chance and explore around to know the town better and to see if he could find new people or interesting jobs. He wanted some new friends at least. Growing up in Daint, he had a few people he hung out with regularly, but when all was said and done, they weren't really what he'd call "Friends," just people whom he had associated with to pass the time.

Steve left his home and went to the Chance gates. The guards let him in, and thankfully the town was a little less crowded this time around. He made sure to get up at the crack of dawn, when people were still asleep. He needed some time to allow the town to show him what it had to offer. His first mission was to stop at this coffee shop that was near the entrance. The shop was a cute little shack with tables outside where people would sip their cup of joe and talk about local gossip. Steve went inside, and the barista smiled.

"Hello, and welcome to Chance Coffee, the freshest cup you can find," the barista said in a happy voice. Then, as expected, "Say, you look familiar. Did you come in a few days ago or something?"

This was the second time that Steve had been asked this, and Steve shook his head. "No, sir. I think you're thinking about someone else. I keep getting asked this, though."

"Oh, sorry. I guess people start to blend together after a while . . . just like our fresh blends. What will you have?"

"Just a cup of coffee, nothing in it," Steve said. The barista rung up the amount, and Steve handed him the coinage. Soon he had a cup of hot coffee in his hands, and he decided to take a sip outside. There were two older men sitting on the benches, and each one had something to say about the town.

"You hear about the new king?" one of the men asked.

"New king? This place changes rulers so fast it makes my head spin."

"Well, they say he isn't related to anyone in the family, if you can call them a family. No one who works outside the castle has even seen him yet. He will be seen during the initiation in a few days, though."

"I hope he's better than the last king. That last one drove the economy a bit south, or so I think."

Steve ignored them and remembered that Chance had a ruler. It wasn't a kingdom, per se, but it was a big town, and the ruler did declare themselves as king. According to some, the king had control over everything, yet according to others, the king was mostly there for show. The family who ran the place founded Chance a long time ago as a beacon for ambitious people to expand their dreams.

Steve sipped on his coffee, savoring the rich flavor and wondering what his next move would be. He could always look for jobs, but right now he was comfortable with learning just where everything was. Even though the coffee was piping hot, he managed to gulp the rest of it down and feel his belly getting all warm. He put his cup away and went down the path that led to more stores. They had a store for everything here—a place to cut your hair, a store that sold shoes and only shoes, a store that had different weapons made of all kinds of material including diamond (though that was a bit out of his budget) and a store that had armor in its display windows. Steve could probably get any job he wanted to, but he would settle on the first thing he saw. Steve was also getting into the residential district. The districts were divided into different houses, from the small poorhouses to large mansions. He passed by this and made his way to the town square.

The town square was starting to get bustling, with people hanging around the fountain in the center. The fountain was of a Creeper that had water coming out of his eyes and mouth. According to the plaque on it, this was built by a servant of the former king who had a sense of humor. He used a Creeper because Chance was "A booming place that was exploding in opportunity." All around, small shops were being set up and children were running around in the grassy patch that was seen as the playground. This was all great, but Steve was busy eyeing the bulletin board that was located close to the fountain.

The bulletin board system was the most famous feature Chance had, even though it sounded like it should have been common sense. Basically, Chance had it so there were bulletin boards scattered around where job hunters could look for new jobs. The one in the square was the most popular one. There was one job on every slip of paper that was tacked onto there, and all you had to do was take the slip of paper to the person who posted the job to apply.

Unfortunately, there were slim pickings, as it was still early. However, there was one slip of paper that caught Steve's eye. "Wanted: Person who can clean the weapons shop. Needs to keep the place free of dust at all times."

Steve wasn't the cleanliest person at home, but he was good at keeping other people's places clean. Steve nabbed the piece of paper and remembered where the weapons shop was. Steve walked toward it, happy about his new job. Maybe he could earn some decent money or even get a free sword. As he went inside, all of these possibilities kept swarming through his head. Chance really was a town of chance.

Chapter Three

Steve went into the weapons shop, noticing all of the displays that were set up. Swords, bows, shovels, pickaxes, all available in different materials that made his head spin. He was wondering where he should start first. There appeared to be no one at the counter, so Steve decided to browse around. There was nothing in his budget, unless he wanted a wooden sword. However, Steve wanted the diamond sword that could cut through anything.

"Need any help?"

Steve looked up and saw a young woman from behind the counter. She had long red hair that went down to her waist, and she had high cheeks that looked prominent when she gave off her employee smile.

"I'm looking for the owner of this shop," Steve said as he handed the paper in. "I'm inquiring about a job posting."

"I am the owner," she said.

What? Steve felt embarrassed and felt like he'd get rejected in no time. He had expected the owner of a weapons shop to be a hairy, buff man, not this woman who was about his age. "Sorry about that."

"Oh, it's fine. It happens all of the time. My father owned this shop, but he was injured in a mining incident and went into an early retirement. I had brothers who should have gotten the torch passed to them, but my father saw me as the one who was the most capable of running this place."

"It looks like you're doing a good job," Steve said.

"Thanks. By the way, did you come in here a few days ago?"

"Let me guess, I look familiar? I've had people keep saying that, but I just moved near here yesterday."

"Oh. Well, this person came in and bought a diamond weapon of everything."

"Not me. I can barely afford a wooden weapon."

She smiled. "Well, sorry for the confusion. I guess you have a rich twin. Oh well, so you're good with cleaning things?"

"Yes, I am," Steve said.

"Well, I'm going to give you a little test to see if you're good for this job. I want you to dust the display cases."

It sounded like an easy job for Steve. Steve was handed a cloth and looked at the cases. They all looked pretty dusty, and Steve wanted to make sure that the display cases were all pristine. He started rubbing against the glass surface, making sure all of the dust was collected from the case. He swiped it around, here and about, until the first case looked like it had been recently made. He did it to all of the other cases until they all looked clean. He looked at his cloth, which looked like a planet for dust now. He handed it back to the lady.

"All done," he said.

"It looks great. I think we have a great cleaner on our hands. Also, do you want to just be a cleaner or do other things for this shop?"

What do you mean?" Steve asked.

"I need someone to do other tasks as well, and I could probably just let you do most of them. You can stock weapons and pick up shipments as well."

Steve smiled. "Sure, boss. Whatever you need done, I'm your man."

"Ha, I like your eagerness. I'm Wendy, by the way. Just call me that."

"Steve," Steve said.

Wendy brought out some coins and gave them to Steve. Steve eagerly put them in his pocket. It was actually a decent amount for dusting a few cases.

"I have nothing else for you today, but tomorrow I have a job that I will pay a lot for. There is a shipment of minerals that needs to be picked up tomorrow. Without them, we can't make any new weapons. The people who gather the materials for us don't take them straight to here because thieves know who they are and what they have, so they try to discreetly give it to people who look ordinary. Your job is to just pick up the materials and bring them here. Got that?"

Steve nodded. It sounded fun, and Steve's heart was fluttering a little bit just thinking about it. He had a job and would be making money to live off of. If this went well, he'd have a great reference if he wanted even bigger jobs. He shook Wendy's hand and left the shop. There was still plenty of time left, so Steve wandered around.

He made his way to the castle, which was pretty expansive and located in the back of the town, resting against the town's wall. A gate was set up, and two guards were in front of it.

"Sorry, but although the castle is usually available for public viewing, we must close it off until the new king is sworn in," one of the guards said.

Steve shrugged. It was no biggie that he couldn't get in, but he was a little curious as to whom the new king was. He decided to just begin walking home. The town was getting even busier, and he was quite eager to see what else it would have to offer. For now, though, he was hungry. With the money he had, he bought himself a meat pie from a stand. He spent the next thirty minutes munching on it on the hill outside of the town. It tasted like heaven. The meat was so rich and flavorful. He then decided to spruce up his house a little bit more. He added more structure, added some more furniture, and made sure everything looked passable for the day. Once the sun began to set, he plopped down on his bed, smiling. In just a day, he had a better job than most people in Daint ever dreamed of having. He knew that it was just going to get better, too. He wondered how his job tomorrow would go, and how he would take care of the supplies. He'd make sure that they were in good hands.

Chapter Four

The day began, and Steve eagerly jumped out of bed as he prepared himself for the adventure that would take place today. He fixed himself a quick bite to eat and headed to Chance, and as he did, he wondered how long this job would take. He was eager to explore and do work, sure, but he wanted time to himself too.

He entered Chance and went inside the weapons shop. Wendy was there, and she smiled as she saw Steve come in. "Just in time. I have the details set up." She handed Steve a slip of paper. It had instructions on where to go and told him to present this to the people who had gathered the materials for her. On the bottom, it had her signature, which looked better than anything Steve could write. "There is no time limit, but I'd like to have them before sunset, if that's okay with you. It should only take a few hours though."

Steve nodded and grabbed the slip of paper, putting it into his pocket. Wendy also handed him a bottle. "Here, it's filled with water. In case you get thirsty. There's also a clean stream close by where you can fill up. The bottle's on me."

Wendy also handed him a steel sword from the display case. "Another thing that's on me. If you encounter hostile mobs or thieves, give them a good slash. You can keep the sword, but if you lose it, I won't give you another one."

Steve grabbed the bottle and sword, thanking her for her kindness, and headed out of there. Steve wanted to give her the goods as soon as he could so he could make a good impression. Not only that but he was eager to try out his new sword.

Coming from a small town, self-defense wasn't needed, so swords weren't all that popular. It was mainly limited to children getting wooden swords to play with. Steve remembered having his own wooden sword all of the time, and he was actually quite good for a child. He remembered taking out his peers quite easily, and managing to do some pretty cool swings. But he accidentally broke his parents' window while playing with it too roughly, so that was the end of his sword. Now that he was grown up, Steve realized that he had to relearn the sword, this time with a blade that was actually sharp.

Steve left Chance and looked at the letter. Directly north from here, about a few miles, there was a mine where the weapons shop got the materials from. That was where Steve would meet the people up at. He set off, but not before practicing with his sword a little bit. Steve swung it around in different directions, trying to get the feel for it again. The sword was a delicate thing that needed to be swung properly, so he did that while walking. He ran into a tree and decided that it would make good practice. He put everything down and started attacking the tree from its side. The sword was actually sharp, and it cut through the trunk easily. The tree fell down, and Steve continued on. His practice was cut short, no pun intended, but at least he was getting the hang of his sword. All he needed to do now was to find the mine where the materials were.

He continued walking, and as he did, he heard some grass rustling. He turned around, only to see that a Creeper was trying to sneak up on him. It's a good thing Steve heard that, or he'd be into pieces. Steve immediately turned around and charged toward the Creeper, bringing his sword down between the creature's eyes before it could even start its infamous hiss. Because of this, the creature fell over without even expanding. He breathed a sigh of relief. He had overpowered the Creeper easily, but unless he was on his toes all of the time, next time might not be so lucky.

He trekked on, feeling the sweat pour down from his brow. It was one of the hotter days, and Steve took a swig from his bottle. He eventually ran across the stream, and he filled his bottle up with that. He took another drink. Ahh, it tasted great. Better than any other kind of water, that was for sure. Now he had to continue on. It had been a few hours, and all he wanted to do was to get the materials and head back and get paid.

He eventually ran into a man covered in rags who was sitting on a rock. He had long, scraggly white hair and a flowing white beard. He stood up, holding himself up with a cane. "Where are you going, sonny?" the old man asked.

"I'm going to get some materials and bring them back to the weapons shop," Steve said. "Why you ask?"

"Just curious. I'm just sitting here, thinking about life, and am curious to know what other travelers are up to. The mine is close, however, so I wish you all of the luck."

Steve nodded and continued on, thinking that the old man, while harmless, was a bit off his rocker. Oh well, the mine was coming up soon, and Steve was glad that his journey was almost halfway over. He saw the ground change from grass to stone and then saw a gated place that had a tall iron fence surrounding it. He could see the mine from beyond the iron fence, and the only way to it was through the gate which led to a building which was being blocked by two guards.

"Halt! Who goes there? This is the Queen's Mine, and unless you have permission, you can't enter!"

Steve took out his slip of paper, and the guard looked at it. "Very sorry for asking, sir. There just has been a surge of thieves around here. Well, right this way."

Steve was led inside of the house and was ushered to a counter. Behind the counter was an older man wearing a suit. A giant sack was placed on the counter.

"Hello, sir, I'm assuming you're the delivery boy. We have an amazing haul for the shop this time. We struck gold and diamonds, so it's mostly filled with that. Deliver it back to the shop."

Steve picked up the bag in exchange for the paper. It was heavy, but it also was somewhat easy to carry, though he'd probably be worn down when everything was over with. Steve thanked the man and carried the sack outside, and as he did, he walked down the path to Chance.

On the way, he encountered the old man sitting on the rock again. "Got anything good in there?" he asked.

"Oh yeah, tons of gold and diamonds. I'm heading back n—"

Steve felt steel pressing against his neck. "Oh no, you aren't. This is mine."

Steve felt the bag he was carrying get lifted off of him, and then the steel was gone. When he turned around, Steve saw the old man was carrying it, a dagger in his hand. The old man grabbed his long beard and pulled it off, revealing that it was fake. He then pulled off his hair, revealing that it was a wig. His posture straightened up, and he no longer looked feeble but instead like a man still fairly young. His hair was tied back in a blonde ponytail, and his rags were taken off, revealing the green tunic underneath them.

"Ha, I fooled ya! I'm Bartholomew, the great thief! I can't believe that disguise worked!"

Steve charged toward Bartholomew with his sword, but then Bartholomew threw something on the ground. Smoke began to rise, and Steve was blinded just enough for Bartholomew to escape.

Chapter Five

"Huh, that Bartholomew is a clever one. He's stolen from us a few times, but to go so low as to pretend he was an old man was pretty good." Wendy was pacing around once Steve had told her the news.

"You're not mad?" Steve asked.

"It's happened every now and then. We've even hired mercenaries to keep the goods safe, and the thieves still steal everything. It's not your fault; I should have told you to be suspicious of everyone."

"Well, now what?" Steve said.

"I guess we pay the company, count our losses, and be wary the next time we get the goods."

"We're not going to go after the thieves?" Steve asked.

"Don't bother. I know where their base is, but there's no way that I would go in there. I don't even know mercenaries who would take them out."

"I can go. I need to make up for what I did. I'm pretty confident in my swordsmanship."

"It's fine. You need to just continue working and forget that ever happened."

But Steve kept telling Wendy about how he should take them out. "We're not going to get rid of the problem by just being cautious. We have to drive them out and make sure they never steal again."

Wendy sighed. "If you really want to, be my guest. But you're too good of a worker for you to just go die like that. I once caught a thief, and he spilled the beans before being arrested. The thieves are holed up in the Crimson Cave, which is a few miles northeast from here. Like the name says, it's a reddish-looking cave. You can't miss it. But don't go, please."

Steve shook his head. "I'm going to go," he said, and he left the weapons shop. He knew that he shouldn't, but he needed to make up for his mess-up. It was just what he had always done. When he made a mess, he cleaned it up.

Steve left town—but not before eating a meal—and set off toward the Crimson Cave, becoming wary of the mobs on the way there. Steve was getting used to swordsmanship by now, and while he wasn't the best, he could handle himself in a fight. He eventually saw the cave ahead of him. It was reddish in tint, like Wendy had said, and it gave off an eerie vibe. As he approached it, he realized that there was no one around. Yet the cave, when Steve went to its mouth, had torches located around it, so it was obvious that there was someone living in there. Steve went inside and down a tunnel, looking to make sure that no thieves would sneak up on him.

Steve thought of his childhood. His parents were light sleepers, so he had to be nimble on his feet whenever Steve thought about sneaking out at night. Even going to the kitchen to get some milk on sleepless nights was an epic adventure. Sometimes he was caught, and instead of not doing it again, Steve would better his technique until he was a ninja at sneaking out. Like the sword, however, Steve hadn't done that in a while. But when he moved his feet and tried to harness his inner child, Steve discovered that it was actually fairly easy to do.

Steve continued walking, and then the torches stopped as the wall ahead of him merged into a dead end. There was no one in this narrow cave, and for a second, Steve thought that Wendy had been duped. Why would the thieves hide in this narrow cave? Then again, why were there torches around here? Something seemed off. Steve examined the wall in front of him, and that's when he noticed that the wall didn't look like it was made of rock but painted to look like rock instead. One of the parts protruding out looked suspiciously like a button. Steve pressed it, and as he did, the wall began to open up like a pair of double doors, leading to another tunnel. Steve followed it deeper into the cavern, only to see another dead end. This time, however, there was a large hole in the ground, and a ladder led down the hole. Steve climbed down the ladder, careful to not make any noise, and he eventually made it to the bottom.

He was quick and nimble, but as he made it to the bottom, he was wary about what was ahead. In a thieves' den, finding nothing was something scarier than running into thieves. They could be anywhere, willing to take Steve out at any time, and Steve had to take them out as soon as possible. As he continued on, he heard footsteps in front of him. Someone was ahead of him, and Steve moved nimbly to see what it was. The thief ahead wasn't Bartholomew, but the sheathed dagger and similar clothes revealed that he had to be with him. Steve brought out his sword and snuck up from behind him. He then swung his sword. *Thwack!*

Steve made sure to hit the thief on the head with the blunt edge on the sword, so he was knocked out. Steve immediately began to undress the thief and put on his tunic, dagger, and other attire. Steve noticed that there was a gag and a bit of rope in the thief's pocket, and Steve noticed a small hole on the side of the wall. Steve tied up the thief, put a gag in his mouth, and stuffed him in the hole. He hoped this disguise worked.

He ventured on, and a thief passed him by. "You must be new," the other thief said. "I heard Bart has got himself a great stash, and he's about to present it to everyone. We'll be swimming in cash before too long," he said.

"Yeah, I'm new. Care to show me around?" Steve asked.

"No problem. Well, the meeting is happening soon, so I guess I'll take you to the part of the cave where everyone is meeting up."

Steve followed the thief and was soon led to a room that was expansive, with a giant rock in the middle as a podium. About ten other thieves were all gathered around, and Steve blended in with them. They were all talking to each other, and then when they heard a voice telling them to be silent, they all listened.

Carrying a large sack in his hand, Bartholomew hopped on the podium. The sack was definitely the one he had stolen, and as the thieves stared at it, Steve hoped that Bartholomew wouldn't recognize him.

"Hello, all. I stole a great stash for you today. I couldn't believe it myself. That old man costume that someone suggested actually worked. Take a look at this."

Bartholomew reached into the sack, and he was carrying a handful of gold chunks, some diamond ore, and a little bit of other materials, including redstone and copper. "It's amazing. We'll be feasting like kings for at least a year or so. And it's all thanks to this gullible boy!"

Steve wanted to shout at Bartholomew, but he kept his cool. He found it ironic that Bartholomew was calling him gullible yet didn't recognize him in a disguise even less convincing. He watched as Bartholomew laid the bag down.

"Now then, I'm going to take this in my room and sell it for a lot of cash when I find the right customer in the black market. In the meantime, you are all dism—"

Someone came running in the room, and everyone turned around. Steve did as well, and he gasped. It was a man in his underwear, and he looked out of it. It was the person whom he had knocked out. How was this possible? Steve had made sure he was tied up well.

"Someone knocked me out and stole my clothes. It's a good thing the rocks around me were pointed, or I wouldn't have gotten out. One of these people is an imposter!"

Bartholomew dropped the bag, and as he did, he said "You didn't see who did it?"

"Nope, hit me from behind." The man looked at the thieves. "And there's so many different thieves who are around that I've lost track of which ones look unfamiliar."

This caused chaos. People were pointing fingers at each other, saying that they were an imposter, and the accused ones proved otherwise. No one tried to accuse Steve, fittingly, despite the fact that he seemed to stick out. Even Bartholomew joined in the accusing, leaving his bag unguarded. Steve thought that this was his chance. He ran to the bag and grabbed it, and before the thieves could see him, Steve was making his way toward the exit. One of the thieves spotted him, and all of the thieves looked at him.

"Um, yoink?" Steve said.

Bartholomew said, "That's the gullible boy. H-how did he find our base? Get him! No, don't get him. He's mine!"

Bartholomew came running. Steve ran away, but the bag slowed him down. Steve held the bag in front of him as Bartholomew took out his dagger. With one hand, Steve cradled the heavy bag, and with the other, he was blocking Bartholomew's blows with his sword. Bartholomew was quick and experienced, but Steve could keep up. Slowly he made his way back to the ladder.

"Just hand it over, and I'll let you go. Sound good?" Bartholomew asked.

"Are you sure?" Steve asked.

"I'm sure. Thieves' honor. Just give it to me, and I'll let this all slide."

Bartholomew was lying; even the most trusting person could see that. Yet Steve realized that Bartholomew thought he was that clever. Steve dropped his sword, and Bartholomew relaxed a little.

"Yeah, you got me. I'll just hand this over . . ."

Thwack! Steve swung the bag as hard as he could and knocked Bartholomew out and then grabbed his dagger from him. He began to climb up the ladder, looking down to make sure that Bartholomew was still out. With the bag, climbing was a struggle, but he could do it. He needed to make up for the fact that he had failed to keep the bag on him, so he kept climbing.

When he was halfway up, he heard something from below him. Steve continued the pace, but as soon as he tried to go faster, someone was grabbing his ankle. He looked down, only to see Bartholomew.

"We thieves are thick, and that includes the skull. Now, hand it over!"

"Or what? I have your dagger. You can hold onto me all you want, but I'm not letting this go!"

Bartholomew reached into his pocket and pulled out something. He held it, revealing that it was a bundle of dynamite. Before Steve could do anything, Bartholomew lit the dynamite with a match and held it up.

"Give it to me, or I blow us both up. Sound good? I'm not kidding around, kid. You made a mockery of me, and you're not getting away with it!"

"Wow, you're pathetic. I thought thieves had honor and were a crafty bunch, but you're a joke." Steve began to shake his leg as Bartholomew kept a tight hold on it. The fuse in the dynamite was going down fast, and Steve didn't know what to do. Suddenly, Steve had an idea. He didn't want to do this, but there was no other option.

"Fine, here's your bag," Steve said, and he let the bag go. It fell down the ladder, and that shocked Bartholomew. So much that he let go of Steve's ankle and lost his grip on the ladder. Bartholomew fell, and then Steve heard an explosion. The ladder shook, and then he felt the cave shake as rocks started to fall. Steve quickly climbed to the top and noticed that the explosion was causing the entire cave to collapse. Steve ran down the corridor, avoiding the rocks, and jumped out of the mouth of the cave. As he did, the entire cave crumbled, and the mouth was closed up by rubble. Steve breathed a sigh of relief.

Chapter Six

"So that's what happened. I'm sorry I lost the goods," Steve said.

Wendy smiled. "Are you kidding? You single-handedly took down a gang of thieves. I don't care if my stash had to be sacrificed for it. Because of this, I don't ever have to worry about those guys ever again. I'm going to pay you some good money when I get it; that's for sure."

Steve smiled, but he was sighing inside. Despite the fact that they were thieves, Steve hoped that all of them somehow made it out of the cave alright. He didn't like the idea of anyone dying because of him.

By the time he went outside, the sun was setting and it was dark. Despite his long day filled with adventure, Steve wasn't tired. Maybe a little exhausted but not tired. Steve decided that his best course of action would be to explore Chance a little more, as this was a big town, and he wanted to see all it had to offer. Steve began to walk away from the blacksmith's and decided to walk toward the castle again. It was still guarded, but he just wanted to look at it. Something about the castle just seemed odd to him. He was interested in the new king because for some reason he couldn't shake off the feeling that something bad was about to happen to Chance. Oh well, he thought as he went down and looked at the water wheel that was located near the corner. This water wheel delivered water to all of Chance, and the water was then pumped to an underground water system located under the kingdom. How bored he must be to be fascinated by that, he thought. Perhaps all he needed to do was just go home and perhaps work a little bit on his house before he decided to go to bed, or maybe he would just plop down and go to sleep. He didn't know anymore, and quite frankly, he was suffering from post-adventure blues. He found infiltrating the thieves' base to be quite fun, and he was wondering if all of his tasks would be as good. Hopefully he could find some more adventure because he had the talent.

He eventually stopped at the park and plopped down on the bench. Why he was here, he didn't know. He watched the night owls as they went about their daily lives, and one of them stopped and looked at Steve.

"Didn't I just see you a few minutes ago?" he asked.

Not that Steve could remember. "Nope, why."

"There's this guy who looks like you, then. He was heading toward the housing district."

Steve's curiosity and his annoyance peaked. He wanted to know who this guy who looked like him was, and his energy was replenished. This was an adventure he could not get behind. He got off the bench and decided to head toward the housing district, which wasn't too far from here.

Steve kept his guard up as he approached it, looking behind, in front, and to the sides. He wondered if this was a wild goose chase. Maybe everyone was seeing things, or there was this guy who had a similar haircut, but nothing more. But Steve, for whatever reason, thought there was something more behind this, something that was, in all reality, a bit suspicious. Steve continued heading toward the district, and that's when he saw someone ahead of him who was wearing a hood. He approached the person and turned to face him.

"What are you looking at?"

It was simply an old man who didn't look anything like him. For a second, Steve breathed a sigh of both relief and disappointment. He began to walk off, and that's when he saw another person ahead of him. Against the moonlight, his eyes almost seemed to glow, and as Steve approached him, he discovered that the person looked exactly like him.

Chapter Seven

The short brown hair, the youthful face, the green shirt, the same build, he really was just like Steve. The only difference was that his eyes were very shiny, almost glowing. That could have been because of the moon, but it freaked Steve out. He slowly approached this person, who was just standing there like a statue, and then a smile spread across this person's lips. According to folklore, everyone had a double of themselves known as a doppelganger. From what Steve recalled, if you looked into the doppelganger's eyes, you'd die. Steve was alive so far, but now he believed in at least part of this urban legend. The doppelganger of Steve's began to suddenly take off.

"Come catch me!" the doppelganger said. Even the voice closely resembled Steve's. Steve started to run toward the person. Steve was never a runner; he did a nice jog now and then, but could never exactly go very fast. But Steve's will cause him to go much faster, yet he still couldn't catch this person. If there was a difference between them, it was that this person could run extremely fast and had athletics to boot. This person jumped over a bench like it was a sleeping cat. This person could hop across stones that were located near the park. This person could even throw obstacles to slow Steve down. They passed a house, and quick as a hot knife to butter, the person grabbed a vase that was sitting on a windowsill. Steve had just gotten close to this person when he threw the vase toward him. Steve ducked, but that slowed him down by just the right amount. The person then ran into an alleyway with a dead end ahead. Had Steve caught him?

Then Steve noticed the ladder that was against the wall. The person climbed it up with Steve following suit. This person could climb like a monkey, but Steve took his time. Eventually, he was on the rooftop, and the doppelganger had been waiting patiently.

"Who are you?" Steve said.

The doppelganger took off, hopping to the next roof. He jumped like he had springs attached to his shoes, getting to the next rooftop with plenty of room to spare. When Steve jumped across, he barely landed on the edge. Their chase continued as Steve and his doppelganger jumped from rooftop to rooftop, and one time, Steve didn't make the jump. His hand grabbed hold of the edge, and he had to pull himself up. By then, this doppelganger had made it to two other rooftops before stopping. Steve didn't know what this person's deal was. Did he want Steve to catch him, or did he just want to play with him? And not the friends-having-fun kind of play, either. Steve felt like he was a mouse in front of a cat that played with its food before eating it. All Steve knew was that they were running out of rooftops. The doppelganger kept jumping until he was heading toward a house in the corner with no other houses surrounding it. Eventually, the two landed there.

"You can keep up, I see," the doppelganger said. Then he unsheathed a sword that was blue in hue. Steve recognized that as a diamond sword. He remembered Wendy saying that someone had bought diamonds weapons who resembled Steve. Steve took out his regular steel sword but wasn't confident with himself. Even if Steve was more skilled, he doubted that his sword would last long if it was struck by the diamond sword. He needed to avoid the doppelganger's attacks and look for an opening.

"But can you keep up like this?" The doppelganger charged toward Steve, who quickly jumped out of the way to avoid being struck. Steve hadn't expected a fight right now, and all he wanted to do was to just go home. He had enough adventuring for one day. The doppelganger was extremely fast, and Steve could barely avoid his attacks. He had little room to actually attack himself, as this person left no openings.

"Why are you attacking me? I just want to know who you are," Steve said.

"I don't think you'd listen to my reasons. All I'm going to say is that a change will be coming to Chance, and you'll be the one to watch it." As he said this, his eyes appeared to shine even brighter. Whomever this man was, Steve was terrified of him. All he wanted to do was just figure out whom he was and why he looked so much like Steve.

"A change? Like what?" Steve asked.

The doppelganger giggled. "You'll find out soon enough. All I'm going to say is that it will be fantastic, and you'll be the one to witness it. Oh, but don't you worry, I have front-row seats saved for you."

This person was out of his mind. Steve charged toward him, but the doppelganger glided away from him, his movements so accurate that it almost seemed ghostly. The doppelganger slashed, and Steve had no choice but to block with his sword. It cracked a little bit as it was hit by the rough diamond surface.

Steve tried to keep an opening, but the person just smiled and said "Okay, I think you get the point. Let's finish this." The doppelganger charged toward Steve, who backed out of the way. Steve felt his feet touch the edge, and he blocked with his sword. That was when the sword shattered into pieces. The doppelganger then punched Steve in the stomach. The wind was knocked out of him, and before he could recover, the doppelganger pushed him off the roof. Steve fell and landed on a pile of garbage bags that someone had threw out of their window. Steve was in pain and felt disgusting, but at least they had broken his fall. He looked up, and he could see the doppelganger peering from the roof, smiling. He looked almost like a monster from this angle, and his eyes were now shining.

"We'll be in touch," he said. He then walked away. There was a ladder right next to the house, so Steve climbed up it. He was in pain and now unarmed, but he had to catch this doppelganger. When he climbed to the top of the roof, he was gone.

Chapter Eight

"Steve, you look terrible," Wendy said as Steve entered.

Steve didn't exactly sleep well. He had tossed and turned all night with the only thing on his mind being the doppelganger and what he had said. Steve was also in pain. It was a little bit better than last night, but he could still feel the punch.

"I stayed up a little late," Steve lied. Why didn't he just tell her what had happened? Was it because he thought that she would laugh at him, or was it because he was afraid to tell anyone? Wendy looked skeptical but smiled.

"You can go home and get some rest if you want to. You deserve it after taking out Bartholomew and his gang. Don't worry about me because all I have to do is ship a few weapons to all of the guards. The king's initiation ceremony is tomorrow at ten, and he wants the guards to be extra armed."

"I could deliver some of the weapons to them," Steve said.

"It's fine. Get some rest, really. You're a hero. And I should be able to pay you tonight for all you've done."

Suddenly, Steve thought of an idea. "Hey, instead of paying me, could you give me a diamond sword?"

Wendy chuckled. "I'm going to pay you a lot but not that much. I might reward you with one further down the line, but the sword you have now should suffice, right?"

Steve didn't want to tell her that his sword was in many pieces right now, and instead he sighed. He wanted to help her out, but all he could think about was getting some sleep. His body needed it, and he kept thinking about just going to bed.

"I'll take you up on that sleeping offer," Steve said as he left. He made his way to his home and plopped down on his bed. A few hours passed, and he managed to get some sleep. He could always use more, but he had enough fuel to make it for one day. So he went back to

Chance and into the weapons shop. Wendy smiled. "I delivered the weapons, so all should be done for today. Just take the day off."

"Wendy, I," he began, but he didn't want to tell her what had happened, not yet anyway. For some reason, he didn't want her to be wrapped up in this doppelganger business. Instead, he just left before she could question what he was about to say. He went and got some food at the restaurant, and the same two old men were talking.

"Hey, I heard that security is going to be extra tight at the ceremony tomorrow."

"Why is that? No one would attack the king, and besides, the king is usually the kind of guy who never needs protection. Who is this new king?"

"I don't know, but the world feels like it's going downhill."

This was depressing, but Steve thought the king had a point. The doppelganger said that something fantastic was about to happen. Was Steve's doppelganger going to attack the new king? No wonder the king wanted security.

Steve decided that he was going to the ceremony tomorrow, and he'd go as early as possible. He needed to protect the king from this person, and he'd make sure he was close to the king so he'd be able to defend him. He didn't care if he was unarmed; he'd find a way.

Steve spent the rest of his day trying to figure out where he could buy a weapon. He then ran into a vendor near the entrance, who was selling a bow with a few arrows included.

"Discounted for the ceremony tomorrow," the vendor said. Steve noticed that they were extremely cheap, and bought himself a bow. For this doppelganger, maybe he'd need a good long-range weapon, as a sword wouldn't suffice unless it was made from diamonds. He also went to the armor shop and bought himself some steel armor. Not the best protection, but it would do for now.

Steve, once he had gone back home, slipped the armor on and decided to practice a little. The armor felt surprisingly lightweight, and all Steve had to do was figure out how to use a bow. He found himself a stump next to his house and put a tin can on it. He had done some archery before when he was a child, but his skills weren't exactly fresh in his mind. Steve made sure that the tin can was resting perfectly on the stump, and then he pointed his bow toward it. He drew it and then fired. It pierced the bottom of the stump. He closed one eye and made sure that his sights were set straight at the can. He fired, and it soared above it. He needed to just concentrate! He aimed again, and this time he kept his position as he stared the can down. He fired it, and the arrow flew through the can. He congratulated himself, and he began to do other activities with the bow, including throwing targets in the air and shooting them down, aiming toward small objects in the distance and drawing a target on a tree. He pretended that they were all his doppelganger. He didn't want to kill him, but he at least wanted to stop him. He missed more times than he could hit, but he still was improving by a lot. By the time that the sun began to set, he wondered if he could do this. All in the while, he wondered what his doppelganger was doing.

He went back to Chance and explored a little bit but couldn't find him. He assumed that maybe he could find him and put a stop to his plans, but no one even remarked that someone who looked like him had passed by. He eventually threw in the towel and went home. He needed plenty of rest, especially if he was going to take out his doppelganger tomorrow. He approached his house, and that was when he saw something on its side. He went to there, and in big red letters, something was painted on the wall.

"IT'S GOING TO BE FUN TOMORROW!"

Chapter Nine

He surprisingly got a good night's sleep. He figured that he'd be on constant guard, considering his doppelganger knew where he lived, but when he hit the bed, he fell asleep. When he awoke, he checked the clock. It was nine. He wanted to leave at least a few hours beforehand so he could get to the front of where the ceremony would be held, but now it would be a struggle.

He ran quickly to Chance, noticing the lack of guards at the gate. The entire town was empty as well. When he went toward the castle, most of the townspeople were gathered around in front of its doors, its gate finally being opened. In an hour, the king would come out of the doors and begin the ceremony. Getting to the front would be difficult, however. The crowd extended to almost the back, and he would have to make his way to the very front. He ran into the crowd, pushing people out of his way. Some casually let him through, and others struggled. A big lady slapped him when he tried to get through her, and Steve just smiled as he continued going through the crowd. Thankfully, no one had freaked out about his bow just yet.

Steve eventually made it to the very front, where people were lining up near the doors. A bunch of guards were against the wall, all armed with pretty powerful steel swords and looking for anyone suspicious. All Steve could do was just play the waiting game now. If anyone jumped in front to attack the king, they'd be his.

The crowd's ruckus died down when someone came out of the door. It wasn't the king but instead an old man who said he was his advisor.

"Now then, our new king wants people to quiet down and be on their best behavior. So if you can, wait patiently. He is about to come out and give his speech," he said. The crowd cheered and then complied with his demands to be quiet. Steve said nothing. He needed to make sure that the king was unharmed, and he kept looking at the roof and around the corners to see if his doppelganger was close by. He wasn't. No one even said anything about his appearance.

Steve heard the doors crack. The king would be coming out soon, and when he was, he needed to be alert. Then the doors opened, and Steve gasped.

The king was wearing a golden crown, carrying a scepter made from a redstone, had golden robes, and had a ring made from diamond on his finger, but that's not what startled Steve. The king was young, had Steve's face, and had his hair. The king was none other than the doppelganger himself. This wasn't right! Not right at all. He began to get comments from people surrounding him, all saying that he was lucky that the king resembled him. But Steve was too startled to say anything. So this was the surprise the doppelganger had in store. It all made sense.

"He's so young!" an older person said.

"I think he's cute," a teenager girl said.

"Those eyes, they're like the sun!" a man commented. Steve heard those comments, but all he could do was stare the king with a dumbfounded look. He then shook it off. He had to do something.

"Citizens of Chance, I'm grateful to be elected as king, and I'm not the kind of person who will ramble on, so I'll make this quick. A change will be coming to Chance. For years, it's been a place of opportunity, but lately it's become saturated with more and more people. As ruler, I promise to expand Chance and make it a real kingdom. Soon we'll form our own country, and then Chance will become a world power."

Everyone cheered, and all Steve could do was not move. He needed to do something about this, but his legs were like gelatin.

It's risky, but you have to do something! Steve thought. He decided that he must take his doppelganger out then and there. He drew his bow quickly, and before anyone could react, he fired it toward the king.

The king quickly pulled a diamond sword out of his robes, and Steve jumped to the doors.

"Looks like we have an assassin, and not only that but he's an imposter too."

Steve quickly fired another shot, but the king blocked it deftly. This person was unreal. A shot that close should have been unblockable, but his doppelganger swatted it away like it was a dying, fat fly. He smiled as the crowd went crazy, and then he told them to calm down.

"Guards!" the king shouted, and all of them went toward Steve. He had nowhere to go. He couldn't fight innocent guards, he couldn't go through the crowd, as they'd rip him to shreds, and he couldn't go into the castle. The guards grabbed him and quickly put shackles on his arm.

"Take him away! Throw him in the dungeon, and then plan the execution!" the doppelganger said. Steve was dragged off, and he wasn't even struggling. He had surrendered.

Book Two – Steve vs. Herobrine

Chapter One

Steve was walking down a dirt road, feeling smaller than usual. As he walked, he looked at his hands. They were small and stubby. There was a pool of water on the ground. He looked in the pool and saw his face. He was just a boy, no more than five. His cheeks still had plenty of baby fat on him, his hair was shaggy and needed a good cut, and his shirt was torn from too much playing.

He looked ahead, and he saw two men ahead of him. They were in armor, and they were carrying someone between them. The person struggled and kept trying to break free, but their grip was too hard. Steve ran to the side of the road and stood in front of the soldiers. The person they were holding onto was him. Same face, same hair, same clothes, same eyes. This Steve looked at Steve and said, "This is all your fault." It sounded so serious, almost adult like, and it shocked Steve. Steve tried to run, but he saw his own face everywhere. The dirt he was stepping on looked like him. The puddles had his reflection, but not his movements. The clouds formed to shape his face. Every one of them was saying the same thing.

"This is all your fault!"

Steve woke up in a cold sweat, his heart racing. Had it been a dream? Well, at least he was back at home in his bed. As Steve's eyes adjusted, he realized that he wasn't at home at all. The bed he was sleeping on was hard and had little cover on it. His room was cramped and had a dirty toilet close to the bed. Bars blocked his exit, and below the bars was a tray filled with food. Steve remembered not eating it because it looked rotten, looking more like goop from a sewer than anything. He was locked up in a cell at the bottom of the castle. Steve had moved to the city of Chance for opportunity, and he had discovered that the new king was a person who looked exactly like him who said he wanted to destroy Chance. Steve had attacked him during the ceremony and ended up being captured. He had been in there for two nights, and tomorrow was the day of the execution. He looked out of the barred window of his cell. The back of the castle led to a cliff, so even if he got out of the window somehow, he'd be falling. It was still dark out; he had gotten little sleep and couldn't fall back into Dream Land.

Steve looked outside of his cell. The guards had all left their posts, thankfully. They had been not so nice to Steve, feeding him suspicious foods, poking him with their lances, and calling him an imposter. Steve still couldn't believe that tomorrow, he'd be dead. He had so much to live for, and tomorrow that would be taken away. The weight of what had happened didn't come to him just yet. He sighed and waited for when it would hit him. The panicking would be fun. For now, he sat on the bed and waited.

There were footsteps coming toward his cell. Great, another guard to harass him. He braced himself, and then that person came into view. She was wearing a hood, and when she pulled it back, Steve saw a familiar face. The red hair tumbled from her hood, and she smiled at him.

"Wendy, what are you doing here?" Steve asked.

Wendy put her finger to her mouth in order to tell Steve that he should be quiet, and then she pulled something out of the sack she had around her back. It was an iron pickaxe. Wendy began to pick at that bars in front of Steve, barely tapping on them so they didn't make much noise. However, they still pierced the bars with ease, and soon cracks began to spread. A small section of the bars crumbled, and Steve crawled out of the space. Steve stretched his arms and was about to open his mouth, but Wendy whispered, "I'll explain later. We need to get out of here undetected."

Wendy reached into her sack and pulled out what appeared to be a suit of armor. "Put it on. You'll look like a guard, and it should confuse them long enough for us to get out. There aren't many guards at this time of night, but they're still around."

Steve slipped on the suit of armor, it fitting snugly around his body. The helmet he had on included a visor. He closed it so that he could hide his face. Wendy then handed him a steel sword. "You're going to need this as well," she said.

Steve grabbed the sword, feeling alive again. They began walking down the dungeon path. The entire place looked dilapidated, with smelly moss growing from the ceiling and dripping a foul-smelling liquid onto their heads. There were some people locked up, but they were mostly sleeping. One person was awake and started to scratch on the bars as they passed by. Steve felt sorry for them, but if they were actual criminals, he didn't want to risk freeing them.

The hallway ended at some stairs, and they climbed them until they were led to a hallway. Now they were in the castle, and it felt so luxurious. All around, chandeliers made from gold hung from the ceiling, beautiful pot torches lit up the room, there was valuable china everywhere, and when Steve looked out the window, he could see a pretty nice view of the town.

Steve saw a few guards walking around the hallway, and Steve tried his best to look legitimate. He straightened his back up, he marched instead of walked, and he held his sword high with dignity. Guards passed him by, but none thought he looked suspicious. Once they were at the end of the hallway, Wendy checked to see if there were any close guards. She looked out of the window, and from there she could see the front of the castle. There were guards surrounding the front, each guarding the doors with their life.

"Drat, that place is loaded with guards. They're all going to ask why you're leaving your post, and we'll be found out in no time. We need to find another way out of here. I've been in the castle a few times. Near the courtyard of the castle, there's an entrance to the underground water system. We could get out from there."

Steve nodded, and they went down another hallway. "The courtyard is close to here."

Steve kind of wished that he could explore the castle a little more, but circumstances prevented that from happening. He was almost tempted to confront the king while he was sleeping, but even while resting, he'd probably be a powerful force to reckon with. As Steve and Wendy went down, they found a huge set of double doors to their left. Wendy pushed them open, and the two were led into an open area of the castle.

"Whoa, this place is beautiful," Steve said as they stepped out. Steve didn't look like it, but he actually had a soft spot for nature. The courtyard was a place of true relaxation, and the moonlight just enhanced it. There was a garden filled with a field of flowers as far as the eye could see, as well as vegetables that looked extremely fresh. In the center of the castle, there was a fountain with a statue of a king. Steve presumed that this was the first ruler of Chance. Water was pouring from his scepter. To the sides of the fountain, two trees provided an umbrella over the fountain, each with succulent-looking fruit on them. Steve wanted to grab an apple, sit on the gold-plated bench that was next to the fountain, and just relax. However, they needed to get out of here as quick as they could. Wendy ran to the corner of the courtyard, where there was a small shed made from silver. Wendy tried to open the door, but it just rattled.

"It's locked," she whispered. "I hate to destroy even more castle property, but it looks like I'll have to." She took out her iron pickaxe again and started to hit it against the lock. Soon the lock shattered, and the door went open. The only thing inside of the shed was an elevator that had chains attached to it. There was a big red button on the side, and as Wendy pressed it, the chains began to move while the elevator started to lower.

"Okay, now can you tell me why you rescued me?" Steve asked.

"I can. Once I saw that king, I could tell that he was trouble. I mean, he went into my shop a few days ago and bought diamond weapons. No royalty would just go to a store and buy weapons. And the fact that he looks just like you is something that's hard to overlook. Tell me, what's the relationship between you two?"

"I know about as much as you do," Steve said, and he began to tell Wendy about the fight he had had with his doppelganger and how he had something "incredible" planned for him and how he said Chance would fall.

"Goodness, I knew something bad had happened when you were exhausted the next day, but I didn't know it was that bad. This is worse than I thought," she said.

"You believe me?" Steve asked.

"Of course I do. First off, I can just tell it. You're a good person and not just because you helped me out with the thieves. This whole week has been fishy."

"How so?"

"First off, our old king passes away. People said he wasn't our best king, but he's probably way better than this guy. But I digress. The former king was in great health despite getting up there. He left behind no children, and usually if that happens, the council has to pick who the next king is going to be. I doubt the council would have chosen this guy to rule."

Steve realized all of the weight that was going on here. It was enough to make his head spin. Did his doppelganger kill the old king? It was a scary thought.

Wendy continued. "I knew it was extremely risky, but I had to break you out of here, because I think that you're the key to solving this mystery. Thankfully, most of the guards know me and my family, and I'm respected by them. All I had to do was tell them I was making a last-minute weapons shipment, and they believed me. I feel bad about lying, and I know that if I'm caught my family's legacy will be ruined, but for some reason, I feel like I had to save you."

Steve smiled at her and reached his arms around her to give her a hug. She accepted it. The weight of what had happened hit Steve. He was about to be killed, and she had gone through all of that trouble to save him. No one had ever been that dedicated to helping him out. Not even his family had.

Finally, the elevator stopped, and the doors opened up ahead of them. They both got out and proceeded to walk down the water channel.

Chapter Two

There were torches that lit up the water channel a bit, but many were either faded or out completely. Thankfully, Wendy had brought a few with her and gave one to Steve. These torches were crafted so that they lit up as soon as Steve held it up. With both of their torches burning brightly, the channel was lit up enough for Steve to make out the tiny details. There were two rails on each side after the ladder that was big enough to walk on, and between them, the water was flowing at a speed that would sweep them away if they fell in. The water looked crystal clear, and so did the channel in general. There wasn't any dirt on the ground, grime on the walls, or anything to contaminate the water. The channel went in two directions, and Steve asked where they should go.

"The channel is designed to clean the water that goes down the drain," Wendy explained. "The water gets cleaned up and comes out of a waterfall where the Crystal River is. It's quite a long fall, though, so we should go the opposite direction unless you want to try to survive jumping off a waterfall. Eventually we should pop out in Chance somewhere."

"Sounds like a plan. I didn't know the channel worked like this," Steve said.

"It's quite a marvel. The king that my grandpa served created this. He was big on technology, and he created a lot of cool inventions via his research staff, this being his best."

Steve nodded, and they went further down. The path split in three places, with small beams connecting them so they could go left or straight.

"This isn't a maze; if we keep going, eventually we should find our way out of here," Wendy said.

They decided to cross the beam and take the straight path. They walked for a few minutes, and as they did, they noticed that the water was starting to get a bit dirtier.

"At the bottom, there are tiny drains that suck out the dirt and everything that contaminates the water," Wendy explained. At first, there was no stench, but as they went down, it started to stink a little bit. Wendy tried to dismiss the smell by talking about other things.

"So are you sure you don't know him?" she asked. "The king?"

"I don't. I come from Daint, so I'm just a country bumpkin trying to move to the big city," Steve said.

"Daint? I don't blame you for moving. I mean, I love small villages, but I've gone there a few times to deliver weapons, and that place looks like it would get old fast."

"Tell me about it," Steve said, trying to remember if he ever saw her come to Daint. He didn't think he did.

The water was starting to reek, its movements stymied by the grime it was packing. Steve didn't want to know what was inside. As they walked, Steve hoped that he could find an exit soon.

"I think there's an exit nearby. I'm imagining where we are based on the direction we are going, and I think it's coming u—"

Wendy stopped, and her skin turned pale. Ahead of her, there was a spider that was scurrying on the rails. Wendy ran behind Steve, grabbing his shoulders.

"What's wrong?" Steve asked.

"I *hate, hate, HATE* spiders! Kill it!" Wendy demanded. It was kind of funny. She went from calm, cool, and collected to insane in just a matter of seconds. Steve wasn't the biggest fan of these arachnids, either, but he could hold his own against one.

Steve unsheathed his sword and ran toward the spider. The spider tried to sink its fangs into him, but Steve jumped into the air and slashed open the spider's thorax. The spider immediately died, its legs twitching. Wendy still looked scared of the creature, too afraid to cross it.

"I'm sorry. They terrify me. I usually hold my own against mobs, but I can't stand the sight of them." She sighed. "When I was a child, my parents took me to the mines to get some minerals out of there. The mines were supposed to be free of mobs, but there was a cave spider that fell through the roof. It bit me before my parents could kill it. Cave spiders are poisonous, so I almost died from the poison. Thankfully, my parents took me home and gave me a glass of milk before I could be consumed. Since then, I've had a fear of them. I don't even want to pass by its body."

Steve went to where Wendy stood and reached out his hand. "Here, I'll protect you," he said.

Wendy seemed reluctant at first, but then she grabbed Steve by the hand. Her hand felt small and callused from where she worked so much. Steve took Wendy past the spider and let go.

"Thanks," Wendy said. "You relieved some of my tension. Now, let's get going."

The two walked further into the channel, and that's when Steve saw a ladder to the left of him. "Is this the way out?" Steve asked. At the top, there appeared to be a lid. Steve started to climb up along with Wendy. When Steve reached the top, he pushed the lid away and could see the night sky. However, the night sky was obscured when he saw a face peer into the lid. It was the face of a guard.

"Found him!" the guard said.

Steve gasped and quickly climbed down along with Wendy. "How did they know? I'm still wearing my armor, for crying out loud!" Steve said as they made their way to the bottom. When they made it to the bottom, the guard jumped down and began to chase them. They ran fast, with Wendy even forgetting the spider's body.

"And to think that Wendy is involved with this," the guard said as they ran. Wendy growled, and they went to where the path split. All of a sudden, two guards appeared from the paths they hadn't gone to yet.

"How did they get there?" Wendy asked as their only choice was to follow the direction of where the water was going. At least it didn't smell anymore, but Steve and Wendy were more concerned about getting cornered. The guards were closing in on them, and their feet couldn't handle much more. Steve was slowed down by his armor, so he quickly threw off his helmet and armor as he ran. Wendy threw her sack away.

Finally, they reached the end of the line. The night sky was ahead of them, along with the sound of a waterfall. There were no bars protecting them from the edge. If they fell off, they would be swept down the waterfall. They decided to run back into the channel, but the guards blocked off both sides of the channel. Steve looked down the waterfall. It went down a great distance and went into a river. Steve wasn't an expert on falling, but he assumed that he could possibly die if he fell off.

"Hello there, Steve. I see the dungeon didn't feel much like home to you."

A person glided past the guards and stood right in front of the two. It was none other than the king, Steve's doppelganger.

"How did you find out?" Steve asked.

The king laughed, his eyes shining every time the pitch of his laugh hit the highest point. "Oh, I know everything. Trust me, not even a great thief could sneak into my castle and get away with it."

Wendy stood in front of Steve, almost as if she could take him on. "My family has delivered the king his weapons for generations, and as someone who has the knowledge of what all of the kings were like, I can say that you're no king!"

The king smiled, showing off his pearly whites. "I didn't know a brat such as yourself was the end-all-be-all in deciding who is and isn't a king," he said.

Wendy looked ahead to see that some of the guards had looks on their faces that seemed to indicate that they were on her side in this situation, with some making subtle nods. The king approached Wendy. "Don't worry, a traitor like you shall be punished."

Wendy still stood her ground, but the doppelganger went toward her and grabbed her by the arm, flinging her toward the guards. Steve immediately charged toward the king in a fit of blind rage. The king pulled out his sword again and brought it down on Steve's steel sword, shattering it.

"You idiot, you know that my sword can shatter yours. Looks like you're mad because I took your girl away," the king taunted. Steve watched as the guards began to take Wendy away, and Steve screamed her name. Wendy was screaming and struggling, but the guards held her tightly and made sure that she didn't break free.

"Don't worry. We won't kill her. She's too valuable for us," the king assured him as they left. "You, on the other hand, I can dispose of. I wanted you to watch as I destroyed this horrible kingdom, but after you attacked me, I wanted you to be killed as the kingdom was watching. However, I see that that's not an option now. I can't let you possibly get away again. This time, I'll kill you right here."

Steve's heart started to pound. He tried to run past his doppelganger, but the doppelganger grabbed him by the throat and began walking toward the edge where the waterfall was. Steve felt the life force coming out of him and noticed just how strong his grip was.

"This brings back memories, though this time the stakes are a little higher. A fitting end for someone such as yourself, though. A rat getting washed out of a sewer. I like this idea. There's so much more I wanted to do with you, however. Oh well, you can't always get what you want."

The doppelganger looked at Steve, and his eyes became so white that Steve had to squint a little bit. "Goodbye, brother," he said. Steve was then flung off, the roaring of the waterfall becoming his lullaby.

Chapter Three

Steve was even younger now, about four or so. He was in a sandbox, playing with someone who looked a lot like himself. Steve kept digging the sand with his hands and stacked the sand blocks to form a fairly nice-looking sandcastle. The other person, who Steve remembered as his brother, prodded the sand and attempted to make his own building, but it ended up looking like just a stacked tower.

"Here, let me show you," Steve said. He proceeded to help his brother by showing him where he should place the sand blocks and how he could make a castle. After that was done, the two looked at their creations.

"I'd like to live in my own castle someday," Steve's brother said.

Steve nodded. "That would be awesome! We could have a fountain made of chocolate, build the walls from sugar, and have servants giving us candy all day!"

"I'll be the king," his brother said.

Steve looked at him skeptically. "But there can only be one king. You can be my jester," Steve said playfully.

"In your dreams!" his brother said.

They ended up debating for a while as to who would be the king of their imaginary kingdom. It sounded so innocent at the time, but Steve just remembered how ominous it now was.

Steve opened his eyes, his eyelids feeling like boulders. He could see a ceiling made from mud and straw. Well, I guess this meant that somehow he was alive, but how? His whole body hurt, but at least he could feel everything. He tried to move his head up, looking around the house he was in. It was a small shack, but it had some personality to it, from the giant fish skull that was hanging from a plaque to various fishing rods proudly hung up alongside the wall. There was a little desk in the corner with a piece of paper on it, and there were various bobs and hooks scattered around in a tackle box close by.

He heard the door open, and someone walked in. It was a middle-aged man whose facial features were barely noticeable due to his thick salt-

and-pepper beard that covered his face. The only noticeable feature that Steve noticed was that he had bright blue eyes that looked kind.

"Oh, you're awake!" he said, his voice sounding a bit muffled by his beard.

"How'd I get here?" was all that Steve could say. His head hurt when he tried to talk.

"You fell from the waterfall. I saw you plop right into the river. It was a good thing I was fishing there, or you would have drowned. I may not look like it, but I'm a great swimmer, and I easily pulled you up to my boat. I usually catch a big one near the waterfall, but this is my biggest catch yet." He started to laugh, sounding more like Santa Claus than anything.

"How long was I out for?" Steve asked.

"About twelve hours or so. I'm the type of person who gets up around four in the morning to fish, so it should be 'round late afternoon by now."

Steve tried to get up. His body felt like it would crumble as his feet hit the ground, but he fought through the pain and stood up. "Thank you so much for all that you've done, but I need to get going. I'm—" His legs gave up on him, and he plopped back on the bed. "Not going anywhere, it seems."

The man walked up to him. "Lemme head back to my house. This is a hut that I use whenever I go on my fishing trips. I think I have a Potion of Regeneration at home. That should fix you right up."

The man left the hut, leaving Steve to writhe in pain, but he was already thinking about what he should do next. He couldn't just go back to Chance without any weapons. There were guards everywhere now, and Steve didn't want to fight innocent people who were just doing their job. Besides that, without a plan to defeat the king, he would just end up getting hurt again or worse.

Goodbye, brother.

His eyes widened as what the king had said came flooding back to him. The king called him his brother. Appearance-wise, it all made sense. He looked exactly like him, so they had to be related. From a logical standpoint, however, it made little sense. He was an only child. He had always wanted a brother or sister, but his parents always had told him that they managed to get a perfect son on the first try, so they didn't want another child. When they said it, they always smiled, and behind the smile seemed like they were secretly nervous about something. However, maybe he was overthinking it.

As he waited, he kept thinking about it some more. Ever since being locked up, he had been having dreams about being a child and having a brother. In one dream, the brother was being taken away, and in the other, he was teaching him how to build a sandcastle, only for them to argue about which one would be king. Was that his brother? If so, why couldn't he remember ever having one?

Another thing he realized that aroused some suspicion was the fact that his parents had said that they only had one photo of him. That was the one that Steve had brought with him. It was taken when he had been about six, which was a bit older than he was in the dream he had where his brother was taken away. All earlier photos were apparently lost in an accident, and they wouldn't explain why. Steve had just given them the benefit of the doubt, but now that he thought about it, there was always something fishy about it.

After a bit of thinking, he decided that his best course of action would be to find out the truth first. He had a feeling that the key to defeating his brother would be to figure out why Steve had lost his memories and what had happened to his brother. Because of this, he decided that he must head back to his hometown, Daint. He wanted to rescue Wendy, but the king said that she would be kept alive. He needed to come prepared.

Finally, the fisherman came back in with a vial in his hand. It was filled with a purple potion. "I keep a good stock of these because the years are finally getting to me, and these pep me right up on days I feel bad. But I think that you'll need this more than I do."

The man handed him the vial, and Steve immediately gulped it down. It tasted bitter, but if it was going to get him back on his feet, he'd take it. Steve felt nothing at first, but slowly the pain was going away, while energy was replacing it. He managed to get up without falling back down, and after standing for a few seconds, he could finally walk.

Thank you so much, Mister . . . ?"

"Call me Jonish. And it's nothing. I rarely run into people nowadays, and I always like to help out the youth when they're in a tight spot."

"How can I repay you?" Steve asked.

"Maybe go on a fishing trip with me sometime?" Jonish asked. "I haven't had a fishing partner for a while now."

Fishing wasn't Steve's forte, but he'd gladly do it. "I will once this is all over," Steve said.

"I would ask you what 'this' is, but I don't want to stick my nose where it doesn't belong," Jonish said.

"Trust me; the fate of a kingdom depends on it," Steve said. He waved goodbye to Jonish as he made his way out of his hut. Once he stepped outside, he didn't recognize this place. He went back in and asked Jonish, "By the way, do you know where Daint is?"

Jonish nodded. "I used to fish at their little fishing hole. I actually got a good catch. Keep heading north. Should take you a few days to get there."

Steve thanked Jonish again and headed out. He would have to lie low for a while because he was unarmed. He didn't expect any danger right now, but at night he'd have to build his own shelter and make sure that no mobs would attack him.

The field didn't change much, and as he walked he wondered how Wendy was doing. He had this strange feeling every time he thought about her, and it didn't have anything to do with the fact that he was worried. When he held her hand, he had felt tingly inside. When she was being taken away, he wanted to attack the guards, even if they weren't bad. Oh well, he thought as he continued. He just hoped she thought the same about him.

Eventually, the sun started to sink, and Steve went to work. All he needed were the basics; he'd just build a shelter, find a bed, and he'd be good. He quickly gathered some wood, grabbed some wool from nearby sheep, and built a shelter from the dirt. He created a crafting table and built himself a bed, a torch, and a door. Finally, he went to sleep, and it was dreamless.

When he woke up, someone was standing over him, a dagger pressed against Steve's throat.

"No one tries to kill Bartholomew and gets away with it!"

Chapter Four

This had to be a dream, though the cold steel against his throat said otherwise. Bartholomew was a great thief who was infamous for stealing Wendy's goods. Wendy had assigned Steve to retrieve a load of minerals, and Bartholomew had stolen them from him. Steve decided to venture to his lair and get them back but lost the goods after he threw them down a deep cave in order to get Bartholomew off of him. He then knocked Bartholomew off of a ladder while he was carrying dynamite. Steve had heard an explosion, and the whole cave had started to collapse. Steve had gotten out just in time.

However, here was Bartholomew, all in one piece for the most part. His clothes were tattered, his blond hair was down and in a mess, and he had a few red marks on his skin. However, he was pretty much fine.

"How are you still alive?" Steve asked.

Bartholomew laughed. "A fall wouldn't kill me. My dagger can pierce through cave walls, and I managed to stab the wall before I went splat and then dropped down. I threw the dynamite up just as it was about to explode. I was still injured by the force of the explosion, but I was alive. The cave began to fall apart, but thankfully I built a few escape tunnels for this very occasion. I had no time to grab the bag of goods, though. My gang showed their true colors. They all ran like chickens while I was still limping about. I managed to get out of there, and since then, I've been seeking my revenge. I just so happened to see you building that shelter and thought I'd be the one to wake you up in the morning. Any last words?"

Without any weapons, Steve was pretty much doomed. How could he get out of this one? He began to rack his brain, and suddenly he remembered something that the king had said.

Trust me, not even a great thief could sneak into my castle and get away with it.

He said a thief couldn't, but he couldn't be so sure. Steve opened his mouth. "My brother has taken over the kingdom of Chance. If you help me defeat him, then you can have a share of the castle's riches."

Bartholomew laughed. "How am I supposed to believe that? You're just making stuff up so I will let you go. Not a chance. If you outsmart Bartholomew, he'll out-sneak you and kill you!"

"Do you think I can make this stuff up?" Steve replied. "Trust me, the entire kingdom's been taken over. I'm going back to my hometown to see if I can defeat him, and if you help me, I will reward you." It was no use; Steve was repeating himself at this point.

Bartholomew, however, seemed a bit less skeptical. "I'm actually a little bit interested in this, if you're not pulling my leg. I've always wanted to rob Chance's castle, but no one in my group ever had the guts to join me. What would I be doing, anyway?"

"Getting me in the castle. If you can, rescue Wendy as well. She's being held captive by the king." He paused and then added "Without her, you won't have any minerals to steal."

Bartholomew chuckled. "I like your sense of humor." He jumped off of the bed. "Fine, we'll make a deal. I'll follow you to Chance. If you're pulling my leg, I'll end you. If you're not, I'll end you after you give me the riches. How does that sound?"

Steve grimaced a little bit. He didn't make a good deal, but Steve nodded. After he defeated this brother, this guy would be cake. He didn't like having him on his team, but if Bartholomew could help him out, that would be much needed.

Bartholomew started to laugh manically. "If this is true, I'll go from that pesky thief who steals minerals to a legendary thief who stole from a castle. I'll be rich and famous, and I'll finally get an even bigger crew. They say that you have to fall in order to rise, so I can't wait to rise to the top!"

Bartholomew sounded full of himself, but Steve just brushed it off. Plus, having some protection from mobs would be useful.

Steve and Bartholomew left their shelters, and as they did, Bartholomew said, "Don't think about running, either. I run fast and can run for hours."

"Didn't plan on it," Steve said, trying to ignore Bartholomew.

While they walked, Bartholomew tried to make some small talk. "Where's your hometown, anyway?"

"Daint, why?"

"Dang, why Daint? There's nothing to steal from that village."

Steve sighed. "Yeah, it's kind of poor, but it's where I grew up."

As they walked, Bartholomew kept pestering Steve about what kinds of treasures the castle had. At first, Steve humored him by telling about all of the fine china, the beautiful gold, the silver, and everything else, but his questions just kept coming. Eventually, Steve could feel his temper rising a little.

"You know that there's more to life than stealing, right?" Steve said.

Bartholomew chuckled a little bit. "Maybe there is, but it isn't the life for me. To me, having a merry band of thieves and stealing valuables is my life."

"Well, why not try to live honestly? To me, it feels rewarding when you work for the greater good in order to get your pay. People like you for that, and it makes you feel a lot better about yourself."

Bartholomew raised an eyebrow, "To me, it's tradition. My parents grew up poor, and no one would give them any work. They noticed how some people were rich for nothing, so they decided to just become thieves to try to steal riches for the undeserving. I was raised into that, and it's just my life. I admit that maybe stealing from a blacksmith isn't stealing from the wealthy, but I just didn't want to risk stealing from royalty."

Steve sighed.

"What?" Bartholomew asked.

"Don't give me that 'It's tradition' nonsense. I've heard that all my life. Everyone always complained about how Daint was a terrible village, but no one bothered to actually do anything about it because it was tradition to stay there." Steve suddenly felt a bit like a philosopher now as he spoke. "Some traditions should be kept, but to me, if they're holding you back or harming people, maybe you should change your traditions a little bit."

Bartholomew looked at him almost as if he was about to turn a new leaf. "You know, I never thought of it that way. Let me think about this some more." When he opened his mouth, he revealed that the leaf was still dead on the ground. "Naw. I'm pretty happy with my life as a thief right now."

Steve wanted to argue some more, but at this point, it was better to agree to disagree. Right now, he just wanted to defeat his presumed brother.

Ssssssssss . . .

"Oh great," Steve said. He turned around, but before he could do anything, Bartholomew had slain the Creeper. It collapsed with one slash of his dagger.

"I've had enough explosions for a lifetime. Not going to get another one," Bartholomew said in his most passive-aggressive voice ever.

"Would you just drop it? I mean, you had the bright idea to try to blow us both up," Steve said.

Bartholomew winced. "Hey, I wasn't thinking. I wanted that stash, and I always carry dynamite on me if desperate times need those desperate measures, you know?"

Steve ignored this fool, and they kept going on. The night passed, and they eventually built another shelter. Two beds were made, with the beds facing the opposite ends. They both fell asleep, though he could barely get any shut-eye. All the time, he was assuming that Bartholomew had one eye open so he could watch him.

Another day passed, and the two talked less and less. Nothing, it seemed, they agreed on. Eventually, Steve ran into a familiar hill. As he approached the foot, he suddenly remembered something.

He had just turned five. He usually spent every sunset on Sparkle Hill, called that because it seemed to sparkle every sunrise or sunset. It was a pretty place to watch the day change into night, and Steve frequently watched with his brother. As the sun set, his brother asked Steve "So, what did you wish for your birthday?"

"I wished for another cake," Steve joked. "You ate most of it."

"Hey, I was hungry," his brother replied. "I wished to become king."

"Hey, it's a hill. We get it. Now can you stop staring at it?"

Bartholomew's remarks made Steve snap out of it. So, they were twins? That made a lot of sense, but how could Steve not remember him ever having a twin?

The two climbed up the hill, and as they reached the top, they looked down on the village. "Look at that heap of mud," Bartholomew said. Steve had to agree. It was nothing but a set of houses, a few gardens, and a few stores, but Steve actually felt a bit of nostalgia for it. He ran down the hill, Bartholomew standing on the top of the hill.

"I'm not even going to bother with this place. I'll be waiting here. Don't try to escape, or I'll know."

Steve looked at Bartholomew and was glad that he wasn't going to be breathing down his neck while his parents hopefully explained about his twin. As he entered, he was greeted by the other villagers. Everyone knew each other in this place, so immediately people said hello. Mr. Davis, the town doctor, said, "Hello, Steve. I didn't know you were back. Come by my place, and I'll give you a checkup." Some people, including Old Man Jent, greeted him with an "I told you you'd be back. City life just can't beat country life!"

Steve knew that there was little time to be chatty. He said a greeting to them back and finally found his house. It was an actually decent-looking wooden house that had all of the rustic vibes to it. There were jars on the front porch where plants grew. There was a small windmill in the backyard behind the garden. Steve remembered being captivated as a child by it. Okay, Steve needed to stop getting distracted. He needed to get to the bottom of this and figure out just whom his brother was. Steve put his knuckles on the door and knocked, his heart actually beating fast for some reason.

Chapter Five

Finally, the door opened up, and a woman was behind it. She still looked very young a cheerful, with high cheekbones and her dark hair in a bun. She wore an apron that had flour slung on it, and she had a flower-kissed rolling pin in her hand. This woman was his mother.

"Steve? Already back, huh? See, your mother told you that you'd be back once you saw that Chance wasn't what it was cracked up to be." She shouted behind her. "Honey, Steve's back!"

Behind her, a man wearing overalls appeared. He had all of Steve's features, except his face was a bit more weathered with age, he was slightly tanner from all of the hard work he did outside, and his hair was starting to go gray.

"Steve? You told me that you were leaving and never coming back unless for special occasions. And last time I checked, it was no one's birthday, nor was it a holiday."

Steve couldn't stand their attitudes right now, and all he said was "Hi, Mom. Hi, Dad. I'm not back for good. I just need to ask you something."

"Well, come in," Steve's mom said. "I'll fix a meat pie, and you can tell me what's on your mind."

Steve agreed and decided to tell them over dinner. He went inside the house, which led straight to the kitchen. There, Steve's mom began to cook dinner. She drained the meat, put it in the pie crust, and put it in the oven. As she waited for it to cook, Steve went upstairs. He went straight down a hallway and to his room. It had been untouched. His bed was still messy, his wooden Creeper doll was still knocked over, and his cabinets were still dusty. All of it was preserved. He left his room and noticed that to the right, there was another room. It was empty except for a single bed. His parents said that this was the guest bedroom, but they never had guests. Could it have been his brother's bedroom?

"Steve! Dinner's ready!" his mom shouted. Steve went downstairs, and his mom was carrying a meat pie with some of the filling coming out of the crust. She always stuffed her pies with as much food as possible, saying that it was best that way. As Steve sat down, he gobbled up his pie while his parents prepared their own. He wanted to eat it all before he asked them about his brother.

They all sat down, and his dad asked "So, what's this thing you wanted to ask us about?"

Steve's heart began to beat fast and butterflies formed in his stomach. Finally, he asked "Did I ever have a twin brother?"

His parents laughed, and this time Steve could practically hear the nervousness. "You're our perfect son," his dad said.

"Yes. Perfection can't have a twin," his mom added.

"Are you sure? Because Chance has a new king who looks exactly like me, except his eyes glow white. He hates my guts and referred to me as 'brother.' Are you sure, S-U-R-E, that I didn't have a brother?"

Now they were beginning to sweat. Steve continued. "I also have been having flashbacks about having a brother." He looked outside the window and saw the old sandbox. It had been emptied ever since Steve grew out of it. "I used to play with him in this sandbox."

His mom was the first to break. As she spoke, her eyes started to tear up. "So, you found out. This was why we didn't want you to go to Chance," she said.

Steve's dad then spoke. "Yes, you did have a brother. Hang on a second. I'll be back." Steve's dad left, only for Steve to stand awkwardly next to his mom. Finally, he came back with a small box. "We kept these hidden under the floor in your old brother's room." He opened the box, and Steve finally saw the pictures he'd been wondering about. The first picture showed Steve's smiling mom holding two babies. The next showed two toddlers playing blocks with each other. There was even a family portrait. As Steve looked, memories came back, though they were still in fragments.

"His name is Herobrine," Steve's dad said.

Suddenly, he remembered everything.

Steve and Herobrine were always the talk of the town. Daint was always happy when new life was brought to the village, and when something as miraculous as twins happened, the town went crazy. They were always showered with gifts, and the townspeople gave them every kind of service, from building them a sandcastle to them getting treated like royalty.

The twins got along pretty well, but they would bicker over the pettiest things just like any other siblings would. Most of the time, it was due to the fact that Steve overshadowed his twin brother. Steve could craft things easily and could do farm work without messing it up. Steve could pick the carrots carefully, while Herobrine would break them while pulling them out. It was trivial, but now that he remembered what had happened, Steve wondered if that was one of the many reasons why his brother now harbored a hatred for him.

Over time, Herobrine became fascinated with the town of Chance. He had heard about it from travelers and kept saying about how he wanted to go someday. Herobrine wanted to be king of the place, but of course that was just a child thinking unrealistically about what he wanted to do when he grew up. As such, the parents laughed joyfully at his ambitions and made sure that they were fed. Meanwhile, Steve was more of the laid-back child, but he sometimes dared Herobrine to do a few things. Like when he dared Herobrine to tease Old Man Jent's dog, Ruff. Herobrine was convinced to poke it with a stick, and he ended up getting chased all around the village for it, eventually getting grounded while Steve took none of the blame. One night, however, this game of daring reached its tipping point.

Daint had its fair share of scamming salespeople. Because it was a small town, the sellers believed that the people were stupid and thought that they'd buy into anything. Steve remembered his parents buying "Creeper Oil" that could apparently cure most ailments, and it just gave the family explosive diarrhea instead. So when Steve and Herobrine saw this ancient-looking woman coming into the village carrying a vial filled with a black liquid, they knew that they were ready to listen to a scam.

"Hello, boys. Do you know what this is?" she asked. Her face was filled with warts, and it made Steve queasy to look at it for very long.

"What is it?" Steve asked.

"An elixir made from the blood of an Ender Dragon," she said. Steve had heard about the Ender Dragon a few times, yet he didn't remember much other than he thought that it was just a silly fairy tale meant to scare kids. She continued. "It's been passed down from generations in my family in Chance. They say if you drink it, it will give you great and terrible powers. I'm old and have no descendants, so I thought I would sell it to someone."

She looked at the boys, all while making a smile that looked snakelike. "I'll give you this vial for just a few coins."

Steve had some coins in his pocket as allowance for doing the chores, and despite him doubting the claims she was making, he agreed to buy it. He handed her some coins, and she handed him the vial and left the village.

Steve kept the vial in his room but didn't want to drink it. While he didn't believe that it would do anything other than make him sick, he didn't want to risk it. He kept it as a novelty, mostly. However, Herobrine kept pestering Steve about him drinking it. "When are you going to drink the blood of a dragon and get your powers?" he asked.

Steve laughed. "Ha, I'll think about it. How about you drink it instead? You, brother, should get all of those powers."

Herobrine shook his head, but Steve kept telling him to. "Come on, you said that you want to be king. Maybe it will give you kingly powers," Steve encouraged.

Herobrine laughed, but then he looked serious. "I'll think about it. Oh, why not? If you're right, you will have to kiss my feet. I like this idea."

Herobrine grabbed the vial from the shelf and held it up to his mouth. "Smells like the eggs when they're rotten," he said. Regardless, he gulped down the vial. When he was done, he began to violently cough. He finally stopped, looked at Steve, and said "Tastes like it, too. But I don't feel any different. Hey, you tricked me into taking it!"

Steve giggled. "You drank it all by yourself," he said.

The night and following day, everything was normal. Herobrine and Steve played together, bickered, and went about their brotherly ways. Eventually, Steve and Herobrine went to bed as if everything was normal.

When Steve woke up, it was still dark outside, but he could see the room perfectly. There were two eyes hovering above his bed, and both glowed a powerful white. Before Steve could do anything, a fist swung toward him. He jumped out of bed and watched as Herobrine's fist hit the bed. The bed instantly broke in two. Steve watched as his brother turned around. He barely looked like Herobrine anymore. He looked like a monster. Herobrine charged at Steve, who quickly ran out of the room and slammed the door. The door flew off of its hinges as Steve looked back. By then, his parents were up and yelling at the two boys to keep it down and go back to bed, but as soon as they witnessed Herobrine stomping down the stairs, they ran.

Steve went to the kitchen, pulling a frying pan out from the cabinet. Maybe this would knock some sense into his brother. As Herobrine approached him, Steve swung the pan. It just bounced off of him, however. Herobrine finally spoke, his voice oozing of pure evil. "That's not going to hurt me," he said. He suddenly snatched the frying pan away from Steve, who witnessed as Herobrine bent the plate as if it were a tiny fork. Steve circled around the kitchen and ran out of the house. The cool night sky appeared, and Steve just kept running, with Herobrine slowly behind him. On the way, Herobrine punched houses and damaged walls. The entire village was soon awoken by this, and they watched in fear as Herobrine was closing in on Steve. An adult ran to save Steve, but Herobrine turned around and punched them in the stomach, knocking them out instantly. He then turned his attention to Steve, who was trying to leave the village. He sprinted like an animal, and Steve tried to get away but didn't notice the rock. Steve tripped over it and fell down, and that's when Herobrine grabbed Steve by the neck.

"You're always one step ahead of me, and you're always getting me in trouble. Now I'll get rid of you!" Herobrine shouted. Everything was turning black, and Steve closed his eyes. However, he felt himself drifting back to consciousness. The grip loosened, and Herobrine's eyes started to go back to normal. He let Steve go and said, "Is this a dream? What have I done? Steve, answer me?"

Steve could only look at him with wide eyes.

After that incident, word spread fast and someone went out of town to contact his friends, who worked every now and then as guards. Soon, two guards appeared at

Steve's family's door. Steve's family was still trying to figure out what had happened. They hadn't punished Herobrine yet because they weren't sure what had happened. The two guards came in and said that they were going to take them to Chance, where they knew of a wizard who could figure out what was wrong with him. Steve never told his parents what had happened, as he didn't want himself to get into any trouble. Steve then remembered the guards taking away Herobrine. Herobrine had said nothing ever since coming back to his senses, and he said little when the guards took him away. Steve's mom protested, but his dad said that this was for the greater good. Steve ran toward the guards, and that was when he heard Herobrine shout that this was all Steve's fault.

Steve was distraught all day. He barely ate, he barely spoke, and he barely moved. This lasted for weeks, and his parents didn't know what to do. Finally, his dad's friend said that they knew of a powerful hypnotist who could seal away memories in children. Steve remembered looking at the kooky-looking hypnotist as he entered the room, a pocket watch in his hand. He made Steve sit down, and he started to move the watch in a pendulum-like motion.

"Stare into this watch, and count to ten," he said. Steve did so, soon becoming entranced. "You will be getting tired before long. When I snap my fingers, you will be completely asleep." He snapped his fingers, and soon Steve was drifting away. However, he could still hear the hypnotist. "Now when I snap my fingers again, you will forget that you even had a brother. You're an only child, and your parents never had another." He snapped his fingers again, and this time Steve knew that he was an only child. "Now then, when you hear my snapping again, you will be awake, and you're an only child." He snapped his fingers.

"The hypnotist said that if you started to learn that you had a brother, the memories would soon be coming back," his dad said.

"We had to tell the whole village never to speak about what had happened, and we had to convince ourselves that it hadn't happened, either," Steve's mom explained to him.

Steve was horrified. He was just five years old. Kids that age had their moments of being complete jerks, but he had convinced his brother to drink something that had turned him into a complete monster. No wonder Herobrine hated him.

"That's also why we didn't want you to go to Chance. We thought that you might discover your brother," his dad added.

"Wait, so what happened to Herobrine? You guys never tried to see how he was doing or anything?" Steve asked.

"We tried to get in contact with the guards, but after they took him away, they went missing. We asked around Chance and the surrounding villages as well," Steve's mom said. Steve did remember them leaving occasionally "For farm supply purposes." Steve's mom continued. "No one had seen a boy matching his description, and neither did the guards. We assumed the worst and thought that they were attacked by mobs."

Steve shook his head. "My brother's alive, and he wants me dead," he said. Steve felt his heart become heavy, but he also felt a little bit hopeful knowing the story about his brother. However, there were still unanswered questions. What happened to Herobrine after that? How had he become king? Why did he want to destroy Chance? His plans made little sense.

Steve's dad was the one to speak next. "What do you plan on doing, son?" he asked.

Steve didn't know. If it weren't for the fact that he had a thief who wanted him dead, he could stay home, and Herobrine would assume he was dead. However, even if Bartholomew wasn't in the equation, he realized that he had to put a stop to his brother and save Wendy.

"I'm going to save my brother," Steve said. "I don't know how, I don't know if I even can, but if I can get him to snap out of it, maybe we could all be a family again."

Steve's mom ended up tearing up once again, and his dad comforted her. "Well, I can't stop you, but just be careful, alright?"

Steve nodded. As he got up, he gave his parents a hug and thanked them. Even if they had kept him from the truth, he realized that he would have been traumatized forever if he had lived knowing that he had done this to his brother. Steve said his goodbyes, but before he left the village, he knew that he had to get himself armed. He went to the weapons shop, where the owner wanted him to have a chat. But Steve told him to just give him a steel sword and some armor. He complied, and Steve paid him. This wouldn't be strong enough to beat Herobrine, but it was good to have until he managed to get something better. He then bought some food from the merchants and some more water for the road ahead. He needed to be the best he could be if he wanted to defeat Herobrine.

As Steve went back up Sparkle Hill, he looked back at his village. He couldn't believe that such as tiny village could hold such an awful secret. As he climbed all the way up, he waved it goodbye.

"Hey, I was getting bored. At least you didn't escape. And don't try to use that sword on me. I've been experienced in this dagger before you even were experienced in sucking a bottle," Bartholomew ranted. Steve ignored him and looked at the village one last time. He vowed that no matter what, he would return to Daint with Herobrine, and they'd all have a nice meat pie.

Book Three – The Ender Dragon Reborn

Chapter One

The city of Chance was looming right in front of him, and as Steve looked at the outline of the castle and the town surrounding it, he began to wonder what his battle plan was going to be. Bartholomew was standing right beside him, both intimidating him and looking at Chance as well.

"This will be the first time that I've ever actually been to Chance," Bartholomew said. "You'd think that a great thief like me would at least go there on occasion to steal, but I've sent a few of my men to steal from there, and they've all ended up getting nabbed by the guards. I want to keep a low profile, you know."

Steve ignored him. He was too busy thinking of a plan. "I think our best bet would be to sneak in at night," Steve said. "This town is bustling during the day, and everyone would recognize me. There are still people at night, but only a handful. We need to keep as low of a profile as possible."

"Now you're thinking like a thief," Bartholomew said. "Maybe you can join me after this is over. If so, I won't kill you."

Steve shook his head. "I'll pass. My house is close by to here, so let's stay there until the night and think about how we are going to do this."

Bartholomew seemed honestly disappointed but agreed to follow Steve. They went straight to Steve's house, and Steve noticed that the message that his brother had sent to him was still there. "IT'S GOING TO BE FUN TOMORROW!" was still on his wall.

"Dang, he really doesn't like you," Bartholomew said. "Are you trying to become the most hated person in the land or something? Because you're winning."

Steve felt some anger building up at this remark, but he tried his best to ignore him and instead thought about his brother. He started to wonder if Herobrine's hatred for him was just the Ender Dragon's blood talking, or if there was more to it than that. There were still many questions left unanswered, and Steve wanted to make sure that they were all answered when this was over.

"Come on," Steve said as he entered his house. Thankfully, his house had been untouched since the last time he visited it. Bartholomew was looking around, and Steve assumed that he was up to no good.

"Trust me, I don't have anything valuable here," Steve said. "Let's just concentrate on the castle."

"Right, so what's your plan?" Bartholomew asked.

"Well, we need to get into the castle, but it will mean nothing if we're not equipped. Herobrine is armed with a diamond sword, so we need to get one if we're going to stand a chance against him," Steve explained. Bartholomew's eyes seemed to sparkle at the idea of a diamond sword, but Steve ignored that. "We're not going to steal a sword, just borrow it for a little while."

"What do you mean?" Bartholomew asked.

"Well, my friend Wendy runs a blacksmith shop that has a few diamond swords in it. She's currently being held captive by Herobrine, so I'm sure that she won't mind at all that I'm going to be borrowing one from there to save her. I don't know what the current state of the shop is like now. Is someone running it, or has it been locked down? All I know is that we need to go in and grab a diamond sword and some diamond armor," Steve explained. When he noticed that Bartholomew was borderline drooling at this idea, he added something. "But like I said, Wendy's my friend, so we're going to give it back to her once we rescue her and defeat Herobrine."

"Hah, if you think I'm going to do that, you really need to get your brain checked," Bartholomew retorted.

Steve decided to ignore him for now and continued with his plan. "Once we get the goods, we need to sneak into the castle. This is where you come in. There's two ways to get there: through the water channel or through the front door. I have no idea if they stepped up security in the water channel, but either way we go, we need to make it into the castle safely. After that, we'll find out where Wendy is being held and free her. Then we shall confront Herobrine."

Bartholomew was nodding. "Should be a piece of cake for a great thief such as myself," he said.

Steve just nodded. "This needs to be done without getting caught. We shouldn't get into confrontations with guards. They're not the enemy; the king is."

"Right. So like a ninja. Got it."

They continued to discuss more specific parts of the plan and brought in a few "What if" scenarios. Steve wondered what they'd have to do if the whole town was heavily guarded.

"Catapult there? I dunno," Bartholomew said.

Steve had to laugh at that, but he sighed when he couldn't figure out what else he could do. Then Bartholomew suggested something else.

"You could always distract the guards while I go in," he suggested.

Steve put his hand on his face, even though that gave him an idea. Maybe that could work to his advantage. The two continued to talk as they discussed further plans. Eventually, the sun began to sink, and a few hours after it went dark, Steve and Bartholomew left the house and stared at the town that was in front of them. As they got close to the gates, they encountered their first problem. Two guards were at the gates.

"They usually let anyone in, but I doubt they'll not recognize me," Steve said.

"Well, why not disguise yourself?" Bartholomew said.

"I don't have wigs and makeup lying around."

Bartholomew snickered. "Well, time to do the old rock trick."

The what? Steve thought as he watched Bartholomew search the ground. He eventually found a fruit-sized rock. Bartholomew ran to the side of the gate just out of the guards' view. Steve followed.

"This is the oldest trick in the book, but it usually works," he said. Bartholomew peered from behind the corner of the wall and threw the rock across the gate. Immediately, one of the guards ran toward the rock, and the other followed suit. Bartholomew quickly hopped in front of the unguarded gate and carefully opened it so it wouldn't make any noise. The two went through it just as the guards returned.

"That always works," he said. "They never go towards the source of the rock, always to where the rock is."

That was stupid enough to work, Steve thought.

Chapter Two

The streets of Chance were relatively empty this time of night, but there were a few people who were walking around. Steve tried to solve that by staying out of lights so no one could get a good look at his face.

On the way to the blacksmith, Steve overheard two people talking. They stood in the corner as Steve listened in.

"So I heard that tomorrow, our king is going to unveil his plan to expand Chance," said one person.

"I hope it's better than the last king's plan. He just brought more people here and didn't make any room for them."

The two passed those people up while Steve thought about what they were saying. Plans for Chance? Knowing Herobrine in his current state, this couldn't be good. He continued down the street, and the two eventually saw the blacksmith's shop. There were no lights coming out of it, and Steve assumed it was closed. As they approached the door, Bartholomew twisted the knob on the door. It didn't budge.

"Locked, huh? Well, no worries. This should be a cinch." Bartholomew took out a pin and began to fiddle with the lock. "Keep an eye out for people," he said. Steve did so. There wasn't anyone close by who was paying any attention to what they were doing. Steve looked at Bartholomew and then back at his surroundings.

Steve heard a *click!* and noticed that Bartholomew had opened the door. The two went inside the blacksmith's, with Steve locking the door behind them. From the look of the interior, it looked like it hadn't been touched since Steve had last been in there. The weapons were rearranged the same way, and dust was beginning to collect on the display cases. While Bartholomew was looking at what they had, Steve was deep in thought. It had only been a few days, but Steve felt a wave of nostalgia about this place. This was where it had all begun. His first job, his first friend in Chance. No matter what, he would save Wendy. Steve went behind the counter and to where the diamond weapons and armor were being held. As expected, the display case was locked.

"I'm on it," Bartholomew said as he started to pick the lock. Steve watched from the door to make sure that no one was coming.

Knock! Knock! Knock!

Someone was at the door. Steve told Bartholomew to work faster.

"I'm trying the best I can," he whispered.

From behind the door, there was a voice. "We've heard reports of suspicious people entering this place. This blacksmith is closed until further notice. Come out quietly, and we won't get aggressive."

"You were supposed to look for people," Bartholomew said.

"I did. No one was looking at us."

The knocking grew louder as Bartholomew worked harder. Finally, they heard a voice say "Come out on the count of three, or we'll come in!"

Steve's mind went into panic mode. "We need to find a place to hide," he said. He noticed that there was a door behind him. They quickly opened it and went inside.

Inside of the door was the storage room. Steve saw crates and bags, and he assumed that they were all of the minerals. They found the closest bag and one that was filled only halfway with stuff. This had mostly gold in it. They went inside of the bag just as they heard the door open from the inside.

They heard the sound of the guards searching, and then there were footsteps coming toward the door. They opened the door, and Steve could hear the guards walking around the storage room. In an instant, the footsteps got real close to the bag that they were in, and then the guard said, "Looks like we got a false report. There's no one here," the guard said.

"Check the bags," another guard said.

Steve's heart began to pound, and even Bartholomew was noticing.

"Nah. That would take all night. I mean, unless the door was unlocked, we have no proof that someone entered. Besides, I was friends with Wendy's family. I don't think they'd respect the idea of us going through their stuff."

The other guard grumbled as Steve breathed a sigh of relief. They waited until the guards left the room and then left the blacksmith. Then the two got out of the bad. Bartholomew was fascinated with this storeroom, but Steve told him to concentrate on getting the diamond weapons. They went back to the main room and opened up the display case. Steve slipped on some diamond armor. It felt so light, almost like a second skin, but Steve could feel its power. Same with the diamond sword. He could swing this around like air, but it felt extremely powerful. Bartholomew grabbed some armor and a sword as well. Finally, they made sure that no one was outside, and they left the blacksmith.

They avoided townspeople and stayed in the shadows. As they did, Steve noticed how the castle was getting closer and closer. Soon they were standing right in front, and they noticed that there were many guards close to the gate. There was also a manhole close to the fence surrounding the castle, but there was a guard in front of that as well.

"What to do?" Steve asked.

Chapter Three

"I guess the manhole is out best option," Steve said while going over his options.

"Probably so. Distracting all of those castle guards is going to be difficult, but getting that one to go away should be easy. But how are we going to do it?" Bartholomew asked. "I don't see any rocks."

Steve started to think about it, and then he had an idea. "Well, why don't we simply try another manhole?"

Bartholomew shook his head. "Nah, I'll do it the traditional way. When the guard gets away, you can go in the manhole."

"Which is?" Steve asked, but before he could do anything, Bartholomew was running to the guard, running so fast that the guard immediately became suspicious. The guard ran toward the direction of Bartholomew. Steve guessed that it was his turn to shine. He went to the manhole, looking to make sure that the guards weren't looking, and then he opened it up and climbed down the ladder. So far, the water channel looked exactly the same as it did when he and Wendy had visited. As Steve walked down, he heard a noise. Bartholomew was climbing down the ladder.

"I managed to get away from him, circle around, and then I went into the manhole," he explained.

"Well, now they'll probably come looking for us."

"Nah, they probably knew that I was just a common thief. They wouldn't think that we're trying to get into the castle," he said.

Steve and Bartholomew walked down the water channel, with Steve trying to remember which way to go. Thankfully, where they weren't too far from where the courtyard was. They soon saw a familiar elevator close by. The two went inside and hit the switch. As they were pulled up, they started to plan how they were going to go about this.

"Well, our first priority is saving Wendy. Even if we defeat Herobrine first, I don't like the idea of Wendy still being in danger," Steve explained.

"Right, save your girlfriend and defeat the king. So, where do you think she's being held?"

Steve wondered that, but he was blushing a little bit over Bartholomew calling her his girlfriend.

"I don't know. The dungeon, maybe? I know how to get there."

Bartholomew nodded, and the elevator stopped. As they walked out, they exited the shed, and thankfully the courtyard was empty once again. The courtyard still looked as beautiful as ever, but if there wasn't time to rest before, there certainly wasn't time to rest now.

The two walked out and into the hallway. Surprisingly, security wasn't too tight. Despite the fact that a prisoner had broken out, it was laid-back. Though that could be due to the fact that Herobrine thought that Steve was dead. But wait a second; didn't Herobrine say that he saw everything? Steve recalled him telling Steve that as an explanation as to why he had known that they'd escaped despite the fact that they'd gotten out without being caught.

Steve didn't want to think about the idea that maybe Herobrine knew that they were in his lair. Instead, they trekked onward and eventually found their way to the entrance of the dungeon. They went down the damp stairs and went down the dark passageway. Prisoners looked at the two, and immediately Bartholomew began to recognize some of them.

"Hey, some of my old crew is in these cells," Bartholomew declared. The prisoners all jovially responded to their leader.

"Get us out of here, boss," one of them said. He was a dirty-looking man with an unkempt beard and thinning hair.

"We should keep our numbers as low as possible," Steve said. "If we get a whole band, we're bound to get caught."

"Or we could create the biggest distraction of all time," Bartholomew said as he began to pick the locks in the cells. They opened up, and before the thieves could come running out, Bartholomew said, "Pretend that your cell is locked. When I tell you to, you can come out. You guys should distract the guards if possible and cause the biggest riot you can. I'll come back here when I need you guys."

They nodded, and then Steve spoke.

"Have any of you guys seen a girl in here? She was then one who freed me," Steve said.

"Nah, not a single lass has come through here since," one of the henchmen said.

"Well, where could she be?" Steve asked.

Bartholomew began to smile. "Well, if you're looking for info, it never hurts to try to force it out of a guard," he said.

"I don't want to hurt the guards, though," Steve replied.

"Trust me, we just need to get him unarmed, and then he'll talk," Bartholomew assured him. "We won't hurt a hair on his head."

Steve didn't like the idea, but he supposed that the best way to look for Wendy would be through a guard. They said goodbye to the thieves and made their way out of the dungeon. As they climbed up, they saw a guard standing on top of the stairs.

"Speak of the devil," Bartholomew said.

"I knew I heard something," the guard said. He ran down the stairs and toward the two. Steve jumped in front as the guard swung his sword. The diamond sword easily shattered the guard's steel sword into pieces. The guard was about to run up the stairs to escape, yet Bartholomew jumped in front of him.

"You're not going anywhere," he said as he pointed his sword toward him.

"What do you want?" the guard asked.

"Where are you keeping Wendy?" Steve asked.

The guard suddenly stopped sweating, turned around, and faced Steve. "Are you Steve?" he asked.

"Maybe I am, why?" Steve replied.

"I hear Wendy every night crying about you. She thinks that you're dead. I used to be best friends with her father, and it pains me to keep her like this. But I'm afraid of the king. He looks like he could cut me in two with just his gaze." The guard was breaking down, and Steve could make out teardrops forming from his eyes.

"Don't worry. Just tell me where she is, and we'll save her," Steve said.

"You don't understand; it's almost as though the king can hear conversations that are going on in this castle. I was grumbling about my job yesterday, and the king called me to the throne room to give me a reprimand.

"Well, we'll take care of the king. Just tell me where she is. It may be your job, but sometimes you have to potentially sacrifice what's comfortable to do the better thing," Steve said.

"She's being held in the north tower at the very top," the guard said. "He's having her create weapons for him and working her like a slave. Please, you have to save her!"

"I will," Steve said as the two passed the guard. The guard ran into the dungeon, clearly upset.

Chapter Four

Steve wasn't sure exactly how to get to the castle, but he could always see the towers from the outside. Separate from the castle, three towers stood on the east, west, and north sides. They were made from ivory and were taller than the castle itself. As the two went down the hallway, they decided to go in the direction of where the tower should be. They circled around a few passageways and saw a door. Steve opened it, and they were led outside again, this time outside the castle.

Ahead of them, a giant tower stood, a stone pathway taking them from the castle to the tower. A fence surrounded both sides of the pathway, and Steve saw a guard at the front of the tower. Because of the tall fences, there was no way around this guard.

They approached him, and he took out his sword. Steve recognized his face. He was one of the guards who had taken away Wendy in the sewers. As he looked at them, he sighed.

"I know you want to get revenge for taking Wendy. I'd take revenge on me, too. Trust me, she's a valuable asset to the guards, and she's being treated horribly. I don't know what to do, though," he said. "I must follow the king's orders."

"Why? This king clearly is a farce. Just let us through," Steve said with some civility. Bartholomew, however, was a little less subtle.

"Let us through, or we'll have to fight. We both have diamond weapons. You will lose."

All of a sudden, the guard fell down, landing on his back. "You knocked me out," he said. "That will be my story, anyway. Now, go and rescue her!"

The two nodded as they opened the door to the tower. Inside, it was covered with polished stone, and there was a spiral staircase leading upwards. The two started to rush up there, and that was when they were stopped.

An arrow whooshed past Steve's head. He looked up only to see a skeleton.

"A mob? In here?" Steve asked. This was unheard of. Could Herobrine command these guys as well? Before the skeleton could draw his arrow again, Steve slashed the skeleton, causing its bones to fall into a pile. They climbed up farther, and as they did, more mobs appeared. Skeletons, Creepers, even spiders that fell from ceilings. Wendy would not like those, that was for sure. Their diamond weapons allowed them to mow through the mobs. Eventually, the stairs ended, and a path to a door was in front of them. However, it was guarded.

They were not guards, though. Instead, two tall figures stood in their way, both so black that they seemed to make the room darker with just their presence. Violet eyes gazed at them, and their heads nearly kissed the ceiling.

"Endermen?" Bartholomew asked.

Steve had seen a few of these creatures lurking around before. They were rare in Daint, but in his travels he had seen a few. According to folklore, they were harmless unless you looked them straight in the eye, and then they would attack. Their gazes at the creatures caused them to approach the two slowly. They brought out their swords. Steve hadn't fought one before, so he didn't know what to expect. As Bartholomew charged toward one, Steve ran toward the other, he brought his sword down on it, and it vanished, a sprinkle of purple where it once stood. Steve turned around, and the Enderman was right in front of him. Before he could attack, he was punched in the face by the Enderman. Immediately, all of the wind was knocked out of him.

Meanwhile, Bartholomew, who had fought a fair share of them in his lifetime, took it out on the first try. He attacked the Enderman and watched as it vanished. He turned around and brought the sword into the reappearing Enderman. It fell over and disappeared in a puff of darkness. He turned around to see Steve, who was still recovering from that one blow. The Enderman was closing in on him to finish him off. Before it could, though, Bartholomew charged toward the Enderman and stabbed it. It exploded, and Steve got back up. He was still hurting, but at least he was feeling a bit better.

"Thanks," Steve said, panting. He hadn't expected that. What other tricks did Herobrine have for him?

The two faced the door, and Steve opened it up. Inside, a wide room with a furnace in the back faced them. Someone was hammering a piece of heated steel, though she was so tired that she was more or less drunkenly swinging the hammer.

As Steve approached the person, he saw that it was Wendy. Her hair was a sweaty mess, her eyes were sunken, and her skin looked dry. In just a few days, she looked thinner as well, almost frail. When she saw Steve, some life returned to her eyes. She stopped what she was doing as she ran toward Steve, giving him a giant hug. She then started to sob.

"I thought you were dead!" she declared. "He put me in here and demanded that I make weapons nonstop. He then threw a bunch of mobs outside to make sure I didn't escape. I'm good at fighting them, but I knew that even if I did, he would come after me. He only gave me breadcrumbs and dirty water to drink."

She stopped crying slightly. "But deep down, I knew that somehow you were still alive. And I was right. But tell me, how are you alive?"

Steve began to explain how Herobrine told him that he was Steve's brother, how he was saved by the fisherman Jonish, and how he returned to his hometown to find out more. All the while, Bartholomew was standing at the entrance. Wendy had yet to notice him.

"And then I ran into Bartholomew. Turns out that he was still alive." Steve pointed behind him. All of a sudden, Wendy gasped.

"What are you doing with that thief?" she asked.

"He kind of tagged along against my will. But he helped me get here, so I can't say that he's been useless."

As Bartholomew came in, Wendy said "I don't care what you've done for Steve. You've been a burden to my business. When this is over, I'll put you behind bars myself!"

They gazed at each other with anger as Steve continued his story. He told her about how Herobrine was actually his brother and how he had come to be. Once he explained it, Wendy stopped being angry and gave him a hug.

"You have to fight your own brother," she said. "That sounds awful."

"I plan on knocking some sense into him," Steve said. "Now that I have you back, let's kick his butt."

"By the way, where did you get your weapons and armor?" she asked.

"From your place. We had to—"

"You're letting him use my precious diamond weapons? You realize he won't give them back?" Wendy interrupted. Her fire was returning, it seemed.

Bartholomew giggled at this, but Steve told him to be silent. "Sorry for doing that, but I had to make sure we were both prepared. Now let's get out of here, and we'll worry about him later."

She nodded and joined Steve as they left. Bartholomew followed behind them, not wanting to unleash Wendy's temper. They climbed down the stairs, free of mobs. Once Wendy saw the spider bodies, she started to freak out again, but Steve held onto her hand as they went down farther. Once they got out of the tower, the guard was still playing dead. Now they just needed to get back in the castle and find—

"Hello, brother."

All of a sudden, the door ahead of them flew open, and Herobrine was standing there, this time in normal clothing. "I thought I'd dress casual since you know who I am." Herobrine unsheathed a diamond sword. "I'm so glad to see that you've survived.

"I know you're not Herobrine. You've been turned into a monster by the Ender Dragon's blood," Steve said.

"No thanks to you, of course. You told me to drink it. But I'm not being controlled by the Ender Dragon. I'm using its power to my advantage. I realize how terrible the world is. It just opened my eyes to it."

"No, my brother wouldn't think like that," Steve said.

"Whatever makes you sleep better. But whatever. As you might assume, I can't let you out of here freely. You're going to interfere with my plans."

Both of them drew their swords at the same time. "You're not going to get away with this," Steve said.

Both of them charged. Being fenced in, neither had much room to fight. Their swords clashed, and Steve was glad to see that he was on an even playing field weapon-wise. But with brute strength, however, Steve could tell that Herobrine was much stronger than he was. He couldn't lock his swords too long, or he'd be overpowered.

"You've grown a bit, brother," Herobrine said. "But you're still no match for the power of the Dragon's Blood. Observe!"

All of a sudden, Herobrine disappeared. Of course, Steve knew this trick from fighting the Enderman. He turned around and attacked the reappeared Herobrine. Bartholomew and Wendy wanted to jump in the fight, but Steve shook his head as their swords clashed again.

"This is between us," he said to them.

"Do you want to hear about what happened to me after those guards took me away? Because I'll tell you everything once I defeat you," Herobrine said.

"You can tell me once you're freed," Steve said. He attacked, and Herobrine parried the blow. Herobrine ducked and tried to sweep at Steve, but Steve jumped backward and then brought his sword down on Herobrine's head.

Herobrine had no time to duck. He was struck with the blunt edge of the sword square in the forehead. Herobrine closed his eyes and collapsed, landing flat on his back.

"Good work!" Wendy shouted. Steve smiled as he approached Herobrine. Before he could disarm him, however, his eyes opened up, and they were brighter than ever.

"I was just holding back. You're tougher than I thought, though, so it looks like I'll have to finish this now."

Herobrine jumped up and charged toward Steve. Steve held his ground as Herobrine swung his sword. As he did, an aura came from the edge of the sword. It was black and turned the blue diamond sword into obsidian. Steve tried to block it, but as soon as the swords collided, Steve's shattered into pieces.

"Yeah, forget this. I'm outta here," Bartholomew said. He suddenly hopped to the fence and began to climb over it.

"Get back here!" Wendy shouted. But she knew that Steve was more important. As she charged toward Steve, she saw that Herobrine's left fist began to have an aura around it. Herobrine punched Steve in the stomach. Steve had armor, but he felt the blow anyway, and he immediately slumped over. He then turned around and faced Wendy, holding his obsidian sword.

Chapter Five

Steve opened his eyes, and as he did, pain surged throughout his body. When his eyes managed to look around, he discovered that he was on the roof of the castle. He tried to move, but he discovered that his entire body was tied up.

"Steve! Are you okay?"

He looked to his left, only to discover that Wendy was tied up as well.

"I've been better," Steve said. "What happened?"

"Herobrine tied us up and then took us to the roof," Wendy explained. "He's gone now. Said that his plan was almost complete."

Steve needed to do something, but he didn't know what. He tried to break free from the ropes, but they constricted him tightly. "Ugh, I can't break out of these," he said.

Suddenly, the two heard footsteps. Herobrine came out of an opening in the roof and approached him. This time, a black aura completely surrounded his body, and his eyes shined even brighter.

"I'm so glad that you can make it," Herobrine said. "The plan to unleash my wrath upon Chance and this world is at hand."

"Just why are you doing this?" Steve said.

"I'll tell you why. Just listen while I tell you the sad tale of what happened to your dear brother after he was taken away."

Herobrine was being taken away by the two guards, who, despite acting like they were going to help him, were teasing him as they walked further along the path.

"They say that this kid tore up a village," one whispered to the other. "How did this little shrimp do that? I don't buy the whole 'He drank a magic potion' story."

The other one replied, "I don't know, I just hope he doesn't do that to us."

Herobrine looked at the two, who, despite their whispering, were being loud enough to hear. "I can hear you two," he stated.

The two guards looked at him, and suddenly they gulped. As they walked down the path, they suddenly started to shake in fear. But Herobrine didn't want to attack anyone. He was already regretting what had happened in the village, even though it wasn't his fault. He watched as he'd chased Steve and destroyed the village, but he couldn't control his movements. He just wanted it to go away, yet with every passing second, he could feel himself surrendering to its power again. First, he felt an intense pain in his stomach, and then his vision began to get brighter. Then he'd lose all control and give himself up to the power.

Destroy them all, *a voice screamed in his mind. It sounded low and almost like it was growling those words.*

Herobrine could feel himself changing, and he immediately tried to run away from the guards. But the guards saw him trying to escape and chased after him. They grabbed his arm, and that was when Herobrine changed. He pulled his arm upward and threw the guard into the air. As he did, the other guard tried to attack Herobrine with his sword. However, Herobrine dodged his blow and punched him in the stomach. The blow shattered the guard's armor and caused him to reel back a little bit. The other guard who was thrown recovered and tried to charge toward Herobrine. Herobrine's eyes started to shine, and as he did, a black aura surrounded him. Two black fireballs formed in his palms. As the two guards tried to attack, Herobrine fired both of them, and they hit the guards in the chest. Immediately, the guards vanished.

Herobrine could feel himself returning back to normal. As his vision settled, he realized what he had done. He wasn't sure if those fireballs had killed the guards or sent them somewhere else, but he hoped it was the latter. He didn't want to hurt anyone, and the idea that he took two lives scared him a little. To add insult to injury, it suddenly started to rain. Herobrine took cover under a tree and began to sob. The second time he'd changed, whatever was possessing him seemed more controlled than ever. The first time, he was like a mindless brute, but now he was starting to form a mind. What if he couldn't change back? What if . . .

"Well, there's a familiar face!"

Herobrine looked up and saw the old merchant lady staring at him, her skin seeming to stay dry and cracked despite the rain. "Did you or your brother drink the Dragon's Blood?" she asked.

"What did you do to me?" was all Herobrine could say.

"I can see that it worked now," the old lady said. "Excellent. All is going according to plan."

Herobrine got up and ran to the old lady, yanking on her. He was weak now, and she was much taller than him; it wasn't exactly an even match. The old lady just laughed as Herobrine kept asking her what was going on.

"I'm just doing what the prophecy said," the old lady said.

"What? What are you talking about?" Herobrine asked.

The old lady turned around, reciting the prophecy almost like a robot. "In twelve years' time, the moon will turn completely black. A child who has drank the blood of the Ender Dragon will grow up to become king, and on the night of the black moon, the king shall raise his arms to the sky and be reborn as the Ender Dragon."

"The Ender Dragon?" Herobrine asked.

"Yes, the Ender Dragon. Long ago, it ruled this world from a dimension called The End. Three brave warriors rose up and slayed it, and one of them, my ancestor, kept its blood as a memento of their battle. My family has been told never to drink it, remembering a prophecy told by one of the Ender Dragon's followers as the Ender Dragon fell. They wanted to throw the blood away, but a force prevented them from doing so. I was the one chosen to deliver the blood to the boy who would become king, and it just happened to be you. And now the Ender Dragon is going to return! I wish I could live to see this day, but as we speak, my purpose is done."

The old lady cackled at Herobrine, and that was when she slumped over and fell to the ground. She didn't move, and Herobrine became scared. He ran away, completely terrified of what had just happened.

Despite the fact that he changed two times in a row, another episode didn't happen for a very long time. Now that Herobrine knew what it was that was inside of him, it was almost as though he could control it. He realized that knowing his weakness was something that kept it at bay. He didn't return to the village but instead was on the run. He was eventually brought to an orphanage by one of the workers who managed to see him walking around one night during a thunderstorm. Herobrine stayed at this orphanage for a few years before becoming adopted by a woman from Chance named Marla.

Marla was a widow whose husband passed away a few years ago. Having no children of her own to raise, so she had decided to adopt. Herobrine loved his adoptive mother. She always had a smile on her face, and her hair was radiant. It made him forget about his old life, and Herobrine thought that he had found peace. He mostly stayed at home, being homeschooled and not getting out much, so he had little recognition amongst Chance.

Herobrine grew up, and he thought that the Ender Dragon would never return. However, Herobrine didn't know that his happy life was about to come to a close. There was a fever being spread around Chance, one that could be fatal if not treated properly. There was an herb, the Colliroot, that would be able to reduce the symptoms and make it so that you could make it out relatively unscathed, but it was rare, according to the king.

Herobrine watched as his mother's condition worsened, and he decided that he needed to do something about it. He searched every market, but the sellers had the Colliroot at such a high price that he couldn't afford it even if he sold his small house. He cried, begged, and pleaded to every shop owner, but they all shook their heads, saying that their profit was more important. Herobrine could feel his anger rising, and for a split second, he could feel the Dragon's Blood returning. He managed to keep his cool, though. Maybe his mother would pull through the fever without the aid. She was still relatively young, and she was a strong, hard-working woman who was always active. She just had to live.

She passed away a few days later. By then, the fever had mostly gone away, and the public was beginning to speculate just how rare the Colliroot was. They only grew in a certain time of year, but according to some of the books he had read, they bloomed in plentiful amounts. Herobrine buried his mother, tears streaming from his eyes. But things were about to get worse from here. The guards said that she had left her home to no one, so they took it away from him. Herobrine was now homeless, and he didn't know the first thing about how to build a house.

Then, he overheard something. Many guards were admitting that the king had a stash of Colliroot, but he kept it only for himself and his servants. Immediately, Herobrine began to wonder if that was true, and curiosity got the better of him. That was when he decided to sneak into the castle. According to some people, it was kept *in the courtyard. Herobrine ventured down into the water channel, avoiding all the guards, and eventually found himself in the courtyard. He managed to find the storage shed, and he broke the lock using some skills he'd learned while he was in the orphanage. Inside of the shed, there was treasure, weapons, and a suspicious-looking bag. When Herobrine looked at what was inside, he saw that it was filled with a white root that he had seen in limited supply at the stores. Suddenly, after all of these years, the voice began to return to him.*

Chance kept these roots from its citizens, and because of this, your mother died. Now it's time to get your revenge. The Black Moon will be in a week. Time to unleash the Dragon.

Herobrine had been cold and unemotional ever since his mother had died, but now a fire exploded in his soul. His brother gave him the potion and ruined his life. This town had taken his mother from him and ruined his life. Maybe it was about time for this world to pay. He could feel the powers returning to him, but this time, he was mostly in control. He wanted to see Chance pay for what had happened.

Herobrine snuck through the castle and went to the king's quarters. Inside, the king was busy preparing bedtime tea when Herobrine went through the door.

"Who are you?" the king asked as Herobrine slammed the door.

"You took my mother from me, and now you will pay," Herobrine said as he approached the king. "She died from that fever, and you had a plentiful supply of the cure," he said.

The king backed away, sweating profusely. "You don't understand," he said. "It's still a rare plant. I had to make sure there was plenty for the ruling powers, and this drives business to us and invites more people and competition to Chance," the king said.

Herobrine didn't want to hear any of this. "That's a load of crap, and you know it. And now, I shall take over this kingdom." His eyes began to glow, and two black fireballs came out of his hands. "Now then, I want you to write a letter saying that you are going to resign as king and leave Chance and that a young man named Herobrine will take your place."

"Never," the king said.

Herobrine shot a fireball, and it soared past the king's head, barely touching his thinning white hair. "Okay, okay," the king said. He went to his desk and began to write a letter, with Herobrine peering down at him. Herobrine wasn't sure that this would work, but it was his best option to becoming king.

As soon as the letter was done, Herobrine read over it, and then he said, "Good work. Now you're no longer the king. So goodbye." Herobrine shot a fireball and before the king could run, it struck him and he vanished as soon as two guards entered the room.

"The king called me here, and when I came, all I could find was this letter." Herobrine handed it to the guards, who seemed skeptical but couldn't disobey the former king.

As rearrangements for Herobrine being declared king were on their way, Herobrine suddenly felt the presence of someone he hadn't seen in a long time. Herobrine, dressed normally, left Chance and saw that his brother was finishing up his house. Herobrine laughed, and that's when his hatred for his brother began to arise, stronger than ever.

Chapter Six

"And so my plans fell into place. I wanted to make you watch as I unleashed the Ender Dragon, but I decided against that once you tried to attack me. I wanted to make sure that you didn't interfere. But I'm glad that you could have made it to witness the rebirth of the legendary dragon."

As Herobrine spoke, Steve kept looking upward. All that night, it had been cloudy, but the clouds were beginning to clear up, revealing that the moon had become dark. It was the color of coal, yet it was easily distinguishable from the night sky. Herobrine turned around and stared at the moon, his arms raised.

Steve still couldn't break free. After hearing Herobrine's story, he wanted to just go up and give his brother a hug, yet he couldn't even do that. What was he going to—

The ropes suddenly loosened, and Steve looked behind him to see what caused it. Bartholomew was standing behind him, holding the diamond sword.

"I wanted to get out of here, but something inside me just couldn't make me do it. So here I am, saving your butt," Bartholomew declared as he cut Wendy's ropes free. Herobrine was too concentrated at the moon to even know what was going on. Bartholomew handed Steve the sword and slipped off his armor, tossing it to him. "Here you go; you need this more than I do." He then added, "I'm supposed to kill you, not this joker."

Steve slipped on his armor and took out his diamond sword. He then ran to where Herobrine was standing. Herorbine had a black aura surrounding his body, and it was growing as he kept staring at the moon. Steve charged at Herobrine, raised his hands toward him, and just as Herobrine turned around, Steve delivered the blow.

Steve wrapped his arms around Herobrine, embracing him in a hug.

"What are you doing?" Herobrine said.

"I just want to say I'm sorry," Steve said. "I was just a kid, but I know that my actions have caused you a lot of grief. Please, brother, stop this madness, and let's go home."

Herobrine could have killed him, but he stood there, a shocked expression on his face. All of a sudden, the aura around him started to lessen, and as Steve looked at him, Herobrine's eyes dulled, almost looking like normal, even though he still had a slight glow to him. Steve looked up at Herobrine. Was this going to work?

Herobrine finally spoke. It no longer sound malicious, and his voice resembled the happy voice his brother had, albeit matured.

"I'm sorry as well. Please, you have to get out of here. It's taken over me, and I don't know how much longer I can hold it."

Steve shook his head rapidly. "No, you can beat it. Just have faith in yourself. The dragon doesn't control you. You control the dragon, and you can tell him to get out of your body."

All of a sudden, Herobrine's aura began to intensify. His eyes began to glow, and suddenly a malicious smile spread across his face. Steve let his arms go as Herobrine tried to attack him.

"So, it looks like he still has some power," Herobrine said, his voice completely changed. "No matter. The Ender Dragon is almost reborn!"

Herobrine stood still, and the aura began to grow even more. Steve got out of the way to avoid it. Herobrine's white eyes suddenly started to change. They turned pink and then into a violet, and their shape became reptilian-like. His skin started to darken, and then his entire figure turned into a black shadow. His shape twisted and turned. He stretched, sprouted wings, grew claws, and suddenly, he was no longer Herobrine. Instead, a dragon stood in front of them all. Its glowing purple eyes stared right at Steve, and its massive wings started to flap as it went in the air.

"What is that?" Wendy asked.

Bartholomew stared at the dragon and said, "Nope, nope, I'm not doing this." He ran away, and the Ender Dragon breathed a black fireball at Bartholomew. He jumped off the roof right before it could hit him.

"Bartholomew!" Steve shouted, and that was when the Ender Dragon rushed toward Steve, attempting to headbutt him. Steve jumped out of the way, grabbing Wendy as he did. The dragon barely missed them, and he began to fly up in the air again, letting out a roar that shook the skies. As he did, the moon began to go back to normal, becoming white once again.

"What should we do?" Steve asked. The Ender Dragon fired a set of fireballs, and Steve and Wendy avoided them as it charged toward them again. It was heading straight toward Wendy. Steve pushed her, and the Ender Dragon's head smashed straight into Steve. Steve was knocked forward. His armor had absorbed the blow, but he was still in a lot of pain. The Ender Dragon flapped over him, opening his mouth to shoot another fireball. Steve rolled to the right, and the fireball missed him. However, this took a lot out of him, and he still was in a lot of pain. He tried his hardest, and yet he couldn't stand. He stared at the Ender Dragon, not knowing what to do. It was still Herobrine, after all. He needed to get him out of there.

The Ender Dragon swooped down, raising its claws as it did. It was about to finish off Steve, and he wasn't sure what he was going to do. He had to get up, or he'd be skewered. Steve exerted all of the energy he could and managed to stand. He then jumped out of the way just as the Ender Dragon was about to swoop down. On instinct, Steve slashed the Ender Dragon's side, creating a gash as he did. Black blood came from its open wound, and Steve suddenly felt awful. But he had to defend himself.

The dragon flapped its wings and hovered above him and let out another roar. All of a sudden, it looked at Steve, and its eyes began to glow a little less. The dragon let out a roar and thrashed its head. It then turned around, and a dark portal opened up behind it. It looked like it could suck out existence itself, with its swirling black matter. The

Ender Dragon flew into the portal, getting swallowed up by it. The portal then vanished.

"Wait!" Steve shouted, but the Ender Dragon was gone. Steve looked as the moon turned completely back to normal. He began to sob quietly, and Wendy approached him. Wendy hugged him hard as Steve began to say his brother's name over and over again. His brother had taken control of the Ender Dragon at the last second, and he had escaped. So there was still hope. But where had the Ender Dragon gone? How could he save his brother? Steve didn't know, and he was sobbing just thinking about it. Wendy comforted him as he continued to cry. Steve eventually wiped his tears from his eyes and stared at the moon. He couldn't stop his brother because he wasn't strong enough. If that had been the case, he would train hard and free Herobrine.

Steve stared at the sky, and suddenly felt a little woozy. It looked like his injuries were finally getting to him. He closed his eyes and passed out as Wendy rushed to help him.

Chapter Seven

Steve woke up and looked at his surroundings. He was in a bed, and a pretty nice-looking one at that. It felt as soft as a pillow yet managed to conform to his body shape quite nicely. The room itself was covered in bright wallpaper, making it look like a girl's room, but it had a lot of weapons hanging from it as well. A sword was hanging above his bed, a pickaxe on the door, and a few others were scattered as well. Steve got out of the bed, his body still aching, and walked out of the room. When he stepped out, he was greeted by Wendy, who had a cup of tea in her hand.

"Thank goodness you're awake," she said. "You were out for a good while." She yawned. "I stayed up all night making sure you were alright."

"Thanks," Steve said, feeling a bit down. "What happened after I passed out?"

"The guards saw what happened from the ground, so they know all about the king changing into an Ender Dragon and him escaping. Everyone's panicking, wondering who the new king is."

Steve still looked sad, and Wendy hugged him. "Of course, I know that you have more important things to worry about. What are you going to do about Herobrine?" she asked.

"I need to learn more about this Ender Dragon," Steve said. "Find out where it came from, where it lives, and how I can defeat it without killing Herobrine."

"Well, the castle library could have the answers you are looking for, but the Ender Dragon, from what I heard, was always dismissed as a fairy tale, something to entertain children who wanted to hear an adventurous story."

"Well, I guess I'll have to look there. Can you get me in?" Steve asked.

"Maybe. The guards know what happened and are currently waiving your charges as we speak, saying that you are a hero. Some townspeople saw it as well, so some will like you. For the most part, however, the guards don't want Chance going into chaos, so they want to keep the Ender Dragon story hushed and say that the king resigned or something."

Steve sighed. Herobrine was gone, and the kingdom was in chaos. Just great. He didn't know the first thing to do besides look in the library, but as they approached the guards standing in front of the gate, the guard said, "Sorry, Wendy. I can't let you in right now. The castle is a mess." The guard sighed. "We need a king who is experienced in age and is kind yet is a common man as well. Someone who isn't afraid to help out a stranger, you know?"

Steve knew that Herobrine was his number-one priority, but he suddenly knew of someone who could be the new king. He began to take off, and Wendy asked where he was going.

"I know someone who can be our king," he said.

"Okay? Well, I'm going to go work at the blacksmith's. See you in a bit."

Steve left Chance and circled around the walls of the castle town, going down a slope as he did. Eventually, he went to a river where the waterfall was pouring fast. At the edge, someone was about to get into his canoe. Steve called his name.

"Jonish!" he said.

Jonish turned around, only to see the old fisherman about to take off. "Why, it looks like you kept your promise. Most people who say they're going to fish with me never do. I suppose they're busy, but can't a man relax once in a while and just forget about life?"

Steve, despite wanting to continue on his journey, couldn't argue with that. He got in the boat with Jonish, and they used the paddles to make their way to the shore. Jonish had a bucket of worms, and Steve grabbed the slimy thing and slid it onto his fishing pole, a little disgusted as he did. Finally, he cast it into the water. The *splash!* as the bobber hit the water, the rushing of the waterfall, the breathing of

Jonish . . . these things felt tranquil and gave Steve a sense of calm that he needed right now. He needed to rescue his brother and defeat the Ender Dragon, but right now he could relax and make sure that he was ready for the battle ahead and . . .

The bobber sank, and Steve began to reel it in. "Get 'em!" Jonish shouted, sounding like he was cheering on a warrior. Steve yanked and reeled in the fish, and it popped out of the water and landed on the boat. It was a huge one, and its flopping shook the boat a little bit.

"Well, that's the biggest one I've seen in a long time," Jonish said. "I usually don't catch any here."

They fished for a little bit before paddling back to the shore. As they got out, Jonish said to Steve, "That was mighty fun. Now then, do you want to do anything else?"

"Do you want to be king of Chance?" Steve asked.

Jonish laughed a little bit. "Doesn't everyone want to be king?"

"I'm serious. Chance has no king, and the people want a king who is a common man who would help a stranger out. I think you're the perfect candidate."

Jonish stroked his beard a little bit, almost as if in deep thought. "Hmm, I'd have less time to fish, but I could build fishing holes for everyone. Okay, I'll bite. Let's see how much of a king I can be."

Steve led Jonish to Chance and went to the castle, where the guard was still standing.

"I think this man could be king," Steve said.

The guard looked at him. "We aren't going to take just anyone as king," the guard said.

"I think that I'd make a great king. For one thing, I'd build a place for kids to enjoy nature, and hire people to take care of it. That would build more jobs. I'd also teach the public about peace and how everyone should work together for a better Chance," Jonish said. The country-sounding Jonish now suddenly sounded dignified, and Steve could see him donning the crown.

The guard looked at him, interested. "Well, we'll add him to the list. It'll be awhile before we pick our new king, anyway."

Steve smiled as Jonish and the guard talked a little bit. He walked away from the guard and went down a street where no one was around. Suddenly, he turned around as someone approached him.

"Well, it looks like we still have a score to settle."

It was Bartholomew. "You promised me riches, and instead I end up running away like a coward from a dragon." He unsheathed a dagger. "Normally, I'd kill anyone who made a fool of me."

Steve unsheathed his diamond sword, and then Bartholomew put his weapon away.

"But traveling with you," Bartholomew said, "I learned a few things. You're someone I can respect. You care about your family and will try your best to save them. And watching your struggle, I have to admit, I bet I can learn a few more things from you." Bartholomew turned around, almost embarrassed. "Maybe I'll go straight and quit thieving. Or just do it more honorably. I don't know. But what I do know is I'm letting you go. For now, anyway. Maybe we'll meet again, maybe we won't, but I'm glad you let me join on your little adventure," Bartholomew said.

Glad I let you join? You pretty much took me hostage! Steve thought. Bartholomew ran away before Steve could say anything else.

Steve walked along Chance's streets, overhearing the two old guys he heard in the beginning.

"I heard the king was a dragon," one said.

"Ha, as if this place could get any more ridiculous. I'm leaving if the next king is secretly a Creeper."

Steve, despite his situation, had to chuckle a little bit. A little bit of humor over this situation seemed to help.

There was just one more thing to do. Steve walked in front of the blacksmith and sighed. He opened it, and Wendy was behind the counter. She was looking lively again.

"Ready, Steve?" she asked.

"Yeah, I'm going to return the weapons that I borrowed. The armor that Herobrine nabbed from me should be somewhere in the castle." He let out another sigh. "I guess this is goodbye. I can't get in the castle at the moment, so I'll travel to look for more information on the Ender Dragon."

Wendy shook her head. "I don't think so. There's no way you can't face the Ender Dragon without good weapons, so I'm coming with you to make sure that you don't lose my diamond weapons again. Besides, after venturing with you and seeing your story, I think I need to go on my own little adventure with you as well. I've worked at this blacksmith for too long. I need a break."

Wendy turned off the lights to her shop and left with Steve. They walked out of Chance, the two saying goodbye to the castle town. A lot of things were plaguing Steve right now, but he wouldn't rest until they were all gone.

Steve's quest to save his brother Herobrine from the Ender Dragon continues in

The Cult: Part One (The Unofficial Minecraft Adventure Short Stories)

Two young adventurers, Steve and Wendy, have embarked upon a quest to save Steve's brother, Herobrine from a fate worse than death. The beginning of their journey has taken them from one great library to another, but they have been unable to find the information they need to free Herobrine.

Dejected, they return to Chance in a last-ditch effort to learn about the elusive Ender Dragon. The only thing they know is that the beast once ruled in another dimension called The End. Legend has it that three warriors slayed the dragon and that one kept its blood. But Steve and Wendy have no clue if there's any truth to the tale; what little information they have found indicates it is probably a figment of a vivid imagination.

For Steve, giving up on the quest just as it is getting started isn't an option. After all, it is his fault Herobrine is trapped within the mighty dragon that is hell-bent on destroying the world. Steve was the one who dared his brother to drink the unknown substance that resulted in Herobrine's transformation. It was his fault that his brother was being forced to endure unending agony.

But guilt is the least of Steve's problems when he encounters a diabolical cult led by the cruel wizard Draven. Long ago, Draven's ancestors were sworn to protect the Ender Dragon. Now, Draven wants to avenge the dragon's death. To do so, he vows to find and destroy the descendants of the three heroes that vanquished the Elder Dragon.

Cunning and evil Draven lures Steve and Wendy into a trap. Will they escape? Can anyone save them or must they save themselves?

CPSIA information can be obtained at www.ICGtesting.com
Printed in the USA
LVOW08s1847140115

422824LV00010B/280/P

8